Also by June Sylvester Saraceno

The Girl from Yesterday (Cherry Grove Collections, 2020)
Of Dirt and Tar (Cherry Grove Collections, 2014)
Altars of Ordinary Light (Plain View Press, 2007)

Dear Joanne,
I really enjoyed how
this took me back
to the South of my
childhood – especially
the church & rapture
references –
Love
Carolyn
Praying for you –

Feral, North Carolina, 1965

Share Your Thoughts

Want to help make *Feral, North Carolina, 1965* a bestselling novel? Consider leaving an honest review on Goodreads, your personal author website or blog, and anywhere else readers go for recommendations. It's our priority at SFK Press to publish books for readers to enjoy, and our authors appreciate and value your feedback.

Our Southern Fried Guarantee

If you wouldn't enthusiastically recommend one of our books with a 4- or 5-star rating to a friend, then the next story is on us. We believe that much in the stories we're telling. Simply email us at pr@sfkmultimedia.com.

SFK
PRESS

Feral, North Carolina, 1965

June Sylvester Saraceno

Feral, North Carolina, 1965

Published by
Southern Fried Karma, LLC
Atlanta, GA
www.sfkpress.com

Books are available in quantity for promotional or premium use. For information, email pr@sfkmultimedia.com.

ISBN: 978-1-970137-81-1
eISBN: 978-1-970137-82-8
Library of Congress Control Number: 2019939531

Cover design by Olivia M. Croom. Cover art: "Tobacco" courtesy of the New York Public Library Digital Collections. Interior by April Ford.

Printed in the United States of America.

For Dylan, Robin, Linda, David, and Julia.

In loving memory of Dwight and Mary Sylvester, junior and senior.

With deep gratitude to the Gray and Sylvester families for their many tales, and the unflaggingly supportive Victor family, to whom I also belong with my whole heart.

Contents

Dare

I watched the white square of Dare's T-shirt slowly shrink and disappear into the wavy lines rising from the blacktop. No way I could catch up to him now, even if I tried. I wanted to yell after him that he was a jerk, but he wouldn't even be able to hear a car horn from this distance. He was headed toward Feral. Traitor.

I hovered over my bike at the end of our driveway, a long gravel U connected at the top by Rural Route 17. By first grade, I had been allowed on the blacktop, but just the part that would connect one end of the driveway to the other. I made a thousand zeroes rounding off those ends, but had long since branched out from that endless loop. I figured out last summer that there were a lot of places you could go if you didn't ask permission first and just stayed out of sight. On the right side of the driveway, I couldn't easily be seen from the house. This way eventually led to the Virginia state line, with a lot of fields, farms, and the Great Dismal Swamp along the way. To the left was Feral. Riding in that direction, I'd be visible from the house, and there was a good chance Mother would see and call me back inside. Besides, even if I could ride that far, what would I do in Feral? Dare and me hated town and those stuck-up city kids. At least I still did, but Dare rode off every morning now to hang out with a bunch of Feral boys.

I guess I didn't hate everybody there. Birdy and the rest of Daddy's people were from Feral. Mother had some kin there, but most of her people were from Georgia, where she had grown up. That's why she talked so country. Birdy never could get used to it. She was always correcting me and Dare so we would talk right. When Mother talked, Birdy just set her lips into a straight line and didn't say a word. If Birdy or any of them saw me in Feral on my bike, they'd be sure to tell.

Then Mother would lay down the law about where I could ride. Not worth the risk.

I gripped my handlebars hard, and sent a satisfying spray of gravel as I peeled out of the driveway to the right. It wasn't even hot yet, but I could see the tar softening where the cracks in the road had been filled in. I pedaled at full speed, past the Sample farmhouse on the right, past their fields on the left with their family graveyard right there in the rows, so the tractor had to skirt around the graves. I could smell the fresh plowed dirt, and every now and then the cut-grass smell of someone's front yard. If I went far enough there was a road that branched off and led to a country store. It was always cool and dim inside. The counter had canisters full of Bazooka bubble gum, Fireballs, and Tootsie Rolls, but the coolers had the best stuff, YooHoos, Orange Crush, grape soda and, in the freezer section, ice cream sandwiches, Nutty Buddies, Fudgsicles. I didn't even have a nickel so I stayed on the main road, heading to a place where there was another turnoff, toward the Dismal Swamp. I had a spot in mind where there was an old picnic table and a big shade tree with low branches. I could plop down there and watch the sluggish water slur by. It was a good spot to sit and think or throw rocks in the water. And it wasn't town, not even close.

I pedaled so hard the rush of air lifted the hair off my neck. Robins looped between pines like they were playing some game. When I got to my spot, I had it all to myself, not a soul in sight. I eased off where the pavement matched up to the dirt path without too much drop-off. Instead of putting my kickstand down, I just propped my bike against the table and threw myself down under the tree. The shade felt good. I looked up through the rustle of oak leaves, the light filtering down made me feel peaceful the way it always did. That leaf-speckled light, like the light skipping all over the dark water, just made a body feel better.

I figure I can't hate him. Dare taught me all the really important things—how to skip rocks, keep from flinching when playing chicken, walk in the woods without making noise, aim down the barrel of the Daisy BB gun, and maybe the most important, how to spy on people. The best thing he ever did was save me from my stupid name, Wilhelmina Mae Miller. He called me Willie and it stuck, so later that's what kids at school called me. I reckon he saved me countless fights.

Last summer Dare read Hardy Boys stories and we concentrated on spying. We'd done it before, tracking Mother and Daddy undetected, even spying on each other. But it got to be time to branch out. We started by going over to the Perry's place after supper when it was just getting dark. They were old and spent most evenings watching TV. We'd prowl around their little house peeking in the windows, tracking what they watched. They didn't talk much. Later we'd review, lying in the front yard, the air heavy with the sweet smell of corn ripening in the fields.

I was the first to notice how Mrs. Perry sneaked candy when Mr. Perry was in the bathroom. As soon as Mr. Perry headed down the hall to the bathroom, she'd head to the kitchen and take down a Whitman's Sampler box from the cupboard, pick a chocolate, pop it into her mouth, then go sit back down on the sofa—all before Mr. Perry came back from the bathroom. I pointed it out to Dare.

"So what?" he said.

"Well it's like she's doing it in secret, hiding something, ya know?"

"Maybe she just don't want to share with old man Perry." He had gotten in the habit, when no adults were around, of substituting "old man" for mister. There was a long silence before he said, "Sailors used stars to tell where they were when they couldn't see land anywhere."

"So what?" It was my turn to not care.

"*So*, if we learn where the stars are in the sky then we'll always know where we are on the earth."

"I already know where I am. In my front yard, near Feral, in North Carolina, in America, on the Earth. That is exactly where I am."

"But if you were on a ship in the middle of the ocean and it was dark and all you could see was stars, then how would you know where you were?"

"Well, I'd still know I was on the ship."

"How would you know where the ship was?"

"You already said—on the ocean." Sometimes he wasn't all that smart, I thought.

"The trouble with you is that you don't know anything, and you don't even *know* you don't know." He got up and walked toward the house. Spying was over for the night.

"The trouble with you," I muttered to the thin air, "is you think you know everything."

A few days later, Uncle Erskine came to stay with us for a while. He was retired from the Coast Guard and had a tattoo of a naked mermaid on his arm. Daddy made him wear long-sleeved shirts when he was at the table, no matter how hot it was, but there were plenty of chances to see it. We could tell that even though Mother loved her brother, she didn't approve of him either, and that cinched his position as our favorite relative. Once when Daddy asked him to say grace he prayed real fast: *Good drink, Good meat, Good God, Let's eat!* Mother cut her narrowed eyes his way, her lips thinned.

"Brother, we don't welcome sacrilege at this table," Daddy's voice was ice cold.

Dare and me were almost purple from holding back from laughing. When Dare couldn't stifle himself all the way and let out a sort of snort, Daddy reached over and rapped his head with a knuckle. We knew better than to lift a fork before Daddy did, so the silent moment lasted a while before supper commenced.

That night I went to Dare's room and we had a contest to see who could say Uncle Erskine's grace faster. We got louder as we sped through it *gooddrinkgoodmeatGOODGOD LETSEAT* until we were falling on the bed laughing and Mother shouted from the living room for us to quiet down and get to bed.

But Uncle Erskine turned traitor on me. He started to just joke around with Dare, not me. One afternoon I walked into the living room and he and Dare were laughing like idiots and he said, "Shush, here comes your little sister. You know that's not fittin' for a little girl's ears, son." I gave him my meanest look, but he pretended not to notice. And Dare, Dare just nodded and went along with it.

When Uncle Erskine finally left, Dare talked about him all the time, about how he was going to join the Coast Guard and see the world. I couldn't beat it, so I tried to join.

"They don't let girls in the Coast Guard, Willie. It's just guys. You get a tattoo."

"So? I won't tell them I'm a girl and I'll get a tattoo. Only not a stupid mermaid with big titties. I'll get a skull and crossbones or something, like a pirate."

"Pirates ain't the same as Coast Guard. They don't even exist anymore, and if they did, the Coast Guard would arrest 'em. And if they found out a girl was on the ship, they'd throw you overboard. Girls are bad luck on ships."

I had a feeling that wasn't true, but he said it with such conviction that I wasn't sure. Who knows what Uncle Erskine had told him in all that talking they had left me out of?

Eventually, though, we got back to sneaking around and spying. Then one evening we saw something I wished we hadn't. Bored with the predictable Perrys, we were lured by the yellow glow from the windows of the next house down the road, the Armstrongs' house. Instead of going on the road, we went through the Perrys' back yard, across the vacant lot, into the Armstrongs' garden, then crept through their backyard, circling around to the front where we could hear a TV on. Some Sundays, on the way home from church, we'd see them cutting back their rose bushes, working in the garden, or just sitting in lounge chairs with their iced teas in hand. Clearly, they had not been to church. Mother shook her head; Daddy looked purposefully, unswervingly ahead. Their disapproval filled the silent car. Mrs. Armstrong had long hair that she wore loose or in a ponytail, not like the other ladies who favored tight perms with enough hairspray to withstand gale-force winds. On this evening, we heard her laugh before we even got to the window. She didn't even laugh like the other ladies. She had a loud, full laugh that sometimes ended in a coughing fit. We located her and her husband in the living room. Mr. Armstrong sat in a Laz-E-Boy recliner with his feet up, staring at the TV, and Mrs. Armstrong walked in and out of the room talking to him. Only a screen in the window separated us from them. The darkness behind us was growing, and the frogs got louder. Any passing car could have seen us there in the spilled-over light from the window. Then Mrs. Armstrong waltzed into the room with only her slip on. Once in a great while I'd see my mother in just her slip, when she was fixing her face or changing clothes. But Mrs. Armstrong was just walking around the house in a short black slip.

"Now what do I have to do to get your mind off that TV, Harlan?" she sort of sang out, like she was talking to a baby.

"Come on now, Bet, I don't get chance to sit back and relax much. Don't stand in front of the TV like that, honey."

"You ain't said a word about my new slip. I thought it was right pretty, got it on sale, too, so don't worry."

"It's nice, honey." Mr. Armstrong shifted in his chair. She was still blocking the TV. Then Mrs. Armstrong started to lift her slip up, pulling it up close to her hips.

"If you don't like it, I won't wear it. Fact is, I can still return it. Maybe I can find something else that would get your attention a little better."

I knew we should scram by the way she was walking toward him, lifting her slip. But my feet stayed anchored. I looked at Dare's face and it was like he was in a trance. Mrs. Armstrong pulled the slip up over her head and dropped it right on the floor. She just stood there in her bra and panties. She didn't even have a girdle on. Then she started kind of dancing and jerking across the floor towards Mr. Armstrong. She put her foot on the lifted leg-rest of the recliner and pushed it down, which threw Mr. Armstrong forward. Then she straddled his lap and pulled his face into her chest. My face felt like it was burning up. Before I even realized what I was doing, I grabbed Dare by his T-shirt and started to run. Broken from the spell, he ran too and soon bolted way ahead of me. When I reached the front yard, he was lying on the grass breathing hard. I threw myself down beside him. We didn't speak for a long time.

Finally, Dare said, "Listen, you gotta swear on the Bible not to tell anybody we were over there."

"You too."

"I'd get the whipping since Mother will say I'm older and ought to know better."

"They won't find out. Nobody saw us."

We lay in silence for a while before I asked, "What do you think happened after we left? I mean, I wonder what Mr. Armstrong did. She just put his face right smack into her titties. . . ."

"Shut up! Just shut up. There's names for ladies that act that way, walking around with their big old titties pushed out like that."

"What kind of names? How do you know? Where have you seen any ladies do that before?" I was as shocked by the sting in his voice as by the idea that he knew anything about ladies that acted that way.

"Never mind. You just better make sure you never act like that."

A shiver went through me. What did *that* have to do with me?

"That's plain stupid. Like I'd have titties that I'd walk around pushing people's faces in."

"You're a girl, ain't ya?"

A dark cord twisted through me, turning to a queasy knot in my middle. I thought of the older girls on the school bus, twin bumps sprouting in their sweaters. The stupid way they whispered and giggled, put lipstick on, and looked in their pocket mirrors all the way to school.

Dare must have noticed the way this was churning through my gut because when he spoke again it was in his soft voice, like when I'd busted my lip or gotten a goose egg from hitting the pavement when we crashed playing chicken on our bikes.

"Look, don't worry about it. You're just a kid."

Normally, if he'd said I was *just a kid* I'd be mad enough to punch him, but I could tell he was trying to make me feel better. Still, my stomach churned. How had *that* gotten connected to *me?* I was used to the idea that he would always be older and stronger but this—this opened up some gulf that threatened everything.

"Come on," he said, "I'll race you to the house."

"You go. I'm looking for the Big Dipper."

"That's easy. . . ." he started to point.

"I know, I know. Just leave me alone." I cut him off and, strangely, he allowed himself to be interrupted. He always had to have the last word, but this time he just got up and went inside, leaving me lying on the grass. It was nighttime dark by then, and I stared up at the sky, noticing that the stars had begun to swim a little. I thought I could feel the earth spin. It gave me that weird off-centered feeling like when an elevator goes up too fast and your guts are out of place. I crossed my arms across my chest, closed my eyes and willed the weight of my body to press more firmly into place while half-thoughts chased around in my head. *I'm me, in my yard, near Feral, like normal, me—Willie.* Then, for no good reason, I popped up and began to spin, turning around faster and faster, eyes open, arms spread out, treetops and sky blurring, until my orbit got erratic and I fell down. Over and over, I staggered back up and continued to spin and fall, spin and fall. Finally beat, I made a drunken zigzag for the front door. When I went inside, there was a good reason I felt dizzy and near sick. But it was my choice, my spinning that did it.

Birdy

Almost every other week in the summer either Dare or me got to spend the night at Birdy's. But with Dare spending all his time with Feral boys, Birdy let me sleep over more than usual. Birdy was so different from Mother and the church ladies that it was like she was another species. She always had her hair fixed nice without any hairspray, and wore bright red lipstick and fingernail polish. I'd never once seen her in a housecoat or slippers, even early in the morning. And even though she was my grandmother, she was prettier than most kids' mothers.

Usually Birdy was indulgent and would sit for long stretches on the porch davenport or living room sofa talking about almost anything with me. It's a project I have, trying to get grown-ups to talk about things they won't tell kids. You have to sneak up on it, come at it sideways—if you straight out ask, they'll send you outside to play, or if it's night time, tell you to say your prayers and get to bed. That's true most of the time anyway.

Birdy had drawers full of silverware, relics from the world when she was young. I'd poke through the drawers while she worked in the kitchen. Sometimes she'd sit down and tell me the story of the silver, explaining what each piece is for, who it had belonged to, and how it came to her kitchen. I was rummaging in one of her rarely used drawers when I picked up a small trident thinking I remembered its particular function.

"This is for eating oysters on the half shell, right?"

"That's the only remaining oyster fork of the set. You wouldn't happen to know how the other ones disappeared, would you? You wouldn't have smuggled them out for mud pies or doll wars by any chance?"

"No ma'am!"

"Well," she sighed, "that is the sole survivor. Lord knows what happened to the set. They were from your great-great grandmother's silver."

"What's this one for?"

"That's just a pickle fork, nothing special. Let's see," she turned it over. "Plain sterling. I don't know where that's from. It's not worth a nickel."

"And this?" I knew already, but I wanted to hear it again. It made her sad, but she would always tell me anyway.

"That's my brother's baby spoon. We both got one when we were born, with our initials on it, a family tradition that appears to have died out." I fingered the intricate curlicues on the handle, spelling out *WAW*. It was big for a baby spoon, but small for a regular one, and very fancy. I waited to see if she'd tell any more of the story. I hoped that if I didn't interrupt, she'd fill in some of the missing pieces.

"He was so handsome. Every girl in town hoped she'd be the one he'd ask to the dances and, later, down the aisle. Every girl in town. He was nice to all of them, but didn't favor one in particular. He was sweet for a boy, always had something pleasant to say. Everyone loved him. And Billy loved to dance. My mother used to say he'd rather dance than eat when he was hungry." She took the spoon from my hand and, sitting down at the table, traced his initials with her pointer finger. She looked at it like she could see him again. Her face got that soft look, like right before sleep.

"Some of the older girls in town even made a big show of being friendly to me. I knew it was only their way of getting closer to Billy, but I still enjoyed their attention. Thing about Billy was he was just as popular with the boys as the girls, just as good at sports as he was at dancing. You'd think he'd have been full of himself, but he wasn't a bit. There wasn't a trace of conceit in him. Mama always hoped he'd be a doctor. She said someone so smart and tender-hearted ought to go into the medical profession. Course, he never lived that long.

Who knows what he might have chosen to do, or which girl would have been *the one.*"

I knew her brother had died, but I realized for the first time that I didn't actually know how. That he had died young, before he graduated from high school, was always so stunning that it seemed to stop both of us.

"Birdy how did he . . . you know, um, what happened to him?"

She looked over at me and her face drew itself back up into its regular lines. She smiled tightly. "Don't worry, little sister. Nothing's going to happen to you or your brother."

"I know. I mean, I hope nothing don't happen. . . ."

"Nothing *doesn't,*" she corrected.

"Um, I hope nothing doesn't happen to us. But what happened to Billy?"

"Sweetheart, you know that. I already told you. Billy passed away."

"Did he get sick?"

Birdy looked like she was going to get up, but then sank back in the chair a little. She looked at me for a few minutes. "It was an accident. There were a bunch of boys, maybe some girls, I don't know for sure. One night they piled in someone's car and drove out to some juke joint down Old County Road, must have thought it was a lark going to a place where decent folk wouldn't go. That was an evil night and a sad one for this family. None of the other boys got hurt, but Billy had breathed his last before they got him home. That place should've been torched long before it was. That was the only time I ever heard my father cry. He was never the same after."

I sat there and let that sink in. I had never heard these details about Billy's death before. I was elated that she let me in on so much of the story, but it still seemed a little hazy. I had always pictured this angelic boy who lived in the big colonial style house on Main Street where Birdy had grown up as someone who simply languished away. But whatever a joot joint was, it didn't sound like anything that would be associated with my white-gloves-wearing grandmother or her sweet brother that everybody loved. I never pictured him in a car, this boy who got a silver spoon just for getting born, this boy whose picture in Birdy's bedroom shows him as a small child in a velvet outfit with a lace collar of all things. In a car. In a car that crashed. But she didn't say it had crashed.

"Did the car crash?"

"Lord, Willa Mae, you're a regular magpie this morning." This time she did get up, taking the spoon with her and turning her back to me at the sink. "He died. I was younger than him, you know. I wasn't with him at the time."

"I know, Birdy." I got up and stood beside her, leaning into her a little. She looked down at me and her face got soft again. "But what did your mama say? Did she tell you what happened?"

Birdy looked out the window over the sink. She had a half dozen bird feeders in the backyard, different sizes and shapes and designs. Some were for bluebirds, her favorite, though she loved her cardinals almost as much. She loved them all except the blue jays. She hated them for their noise and meanness.

"My mama didn't think it right to speak of such things. Maybe that's something we should be working on with you, Willa Mae. I sure hope you don't ask so many questions when you're visiting folks."

"I wouldn't. It's just that you're my family and Billy would have been my family too. He would have been my. . . ." I couldn't figure out the right relation.

"Your grand-uncle. Just like your Aunt Gertie is actually your grand-aunt because she's Papa's sister, not your daddy's sister."

"Oh." I had almost forgotten the question that I still didn't have the answer for, then I remembered. "So, he would have been my grand-uncle, but he died in a car crash?"

"He died in an accident. I told you that already. Now get those utensils put back away where they belong."

As I was putting away the relish spoons, oyster fork, and other artifacts of her mysterious past, I remembered Birdy had scrapbooks with newspaper clippings of everything that had to do with the family. Her own birth announcement, as well as her brother's, William Ashby Willoughby, was in one, and her engagement announcement, wedding picture, and her mother's obituary. Billy's death notice, too, must be in one.

She was drying the last dishes in the drain and putting them away.

"Birdy?"

"Yes, sweetheart?" she said absently, her mind already somewhere far away.

"Could we go through one of your albums?"

"Could we what?" She looked down at me.

"Could we go through one of your albums and you can show me your wedding picture in the paper?" She knew I loved this, and I knew she did, too.

"Well, I hadn't planned on doing that. I need to go to the store to pick up a few things for dinner." Birdy called supper *dinner* and dinner *lunch* like a lot of town folks did.

"I'll help you."

She laughed. "Well, that's sweet of you. I guess we could take it down for one peek before shopping."

"Then we can look at Billy's stuff, too." I tried to sound casual.

Her face tightened and she drew her lips into a thin line that caused a knot to form in my belly.

"You know, sometimes you should just let things go, Wilhelmina Mae. You just don't know when to stop, do you? Any idea of decency and discretion is just a foreign notion to you, isn't it? Do you know what a busybody is? Well, you're just about to become one. And that would be a sad mistake, let me tell you. No one likes a busybody."

Birdy turned away sharply and went to her bathroom where she clicked the door firmly shut behind her. My mouth felt dry. She was mad at me for being nosy. I went to the living room and sat on the sofa the way she always told me to sit, with my back straight and my legs together. I was hoping that would make things a little better when she came out. But she didn't come out for a long time. I thought about knocking on the door, but I knew that would make things worse. So, I sat. When I felt my eyes stinging, I bit my lip hard to hold back from crying. Then I dug my nails into my palms and that helped.

When she finally came out after what seemed like eternity, her bright red lipstick was darker and I could smell her perfume. She was ready to go to the grocery store.

"I'm sorry, Birdy." As soon as I said it, the tears I'd held back flooded.

She came over and sat beside me putting her arm around my shoulders. I didn't want to mess up her dress, so I kept my face forward and wiped under my nose with my sleeve, knowing immediately that I shouldn't have. She was mild about it.

"Go get yourself some Kleenexes and come sit back down," she said gently. "You know better than to wipe your nose on your sleeve."

I did as she said and sat down, a little less teary-eyed.

"I accept your apology. There's no need to cry." She put her arm back around me and we sat quietly for a while.

"Before we go to the store, I want to tell you something. You're getting to be a little older now and you're out visiting a little more. People are not going to appreciate your curiosity about their private lives, Willa Mae. Much as you like to think everything's a story for you to hear, folks are not going to want you prying into every little detail that catches your interest. You understand what I'm saying?"

She looked intently at me. I didn't understand, but I thought I'd better act like I did. It seemed important to her.

I nodded my head and mumbled, "Yes ma'am."

"Well, I hope you do. There's a lot more that ought to be left unsaid than ought to be said, and decent folks know which is which."

I swallowed hard. I was pretty sure I didn't know which was which, but I did know not having good manners was one of the worst things in the world to Birdy, the same way that sin was to Mother and Daddy. She got more upset when we said *ain't* or slurped at the table than if we forgot to say our bedtime prayers.

"Well, I don't ever plan to be rude, Birdy," I said, and I really meant it.

She practically beamed. I could breathe all the way in then.

"Oh, I knew you'd understand, sweetheart. You are such a bright girl. I'm going to let you pick out one treat for yourself at the store, and also something to take home to Dare, something that won't melt." She gave me a quick hug and went to get her pocketbook and keys.

I felt the relief of stumbling onto the right thing to say for the first time I could ever remember and thought *if only I can keep my mouth shut for the rest of the day, I'll be just fine.*

Shooting for the Lead

The summer Mrs. Armstrong stripped down was also the summer we decided to build a stadium in the yard and hold our own Olympic Games. Dare climbed up on the freezer in the garage to lift the bamboo poles down from the racks while I fished through Daddy's toolbox for a hammer and some nails.

"The two trees on the side yard are close enough together to make a high jump with this pole," he said, pulling out the longest one. "The others can be javelins."

I was ready to start hammering, but Dare was more precise, as usual, and had to get the measuring tape out.

"They have to match up right or it won't work. First, we'll mark off some easy jumps," he said, scoring the first tree with his pocket knife. "Then we'll raise them higher and higher."

He went about measuring both trees and scoring where the nails should go while I rooted around in the grass for four leaf clovers. Then he started to hammer in a nail.

"Hey! Wait a minute! You said I could hammer!"

"OK, OK. Don't make such a big deal out of it. You can hammer next."

I hammered in the rest of the nails while he surveyed areas for the long jump, javelin throw, and shot put. My arrhythmic pounding provoked escalating caws from the jays. An old bedspread became the gymnastics pad, its surface pimpled from the grass underneath. We marked off courses for sprints and long distance runs, found the soft ball that would serve as a shot put, and gathered pine needles for the high jump landing.

It was nearly suppertime before we had the entire Olympic field set up, but finally we could start competing. Dare won five gold medals. I won one. He was older, faster, stronger. But his long legs, such an advantage in the foot races and long jumps, worked against him on the high jump. We raised the bar three times together, but on the fourth bar, his heel trailed and knocked the pole off the carefully set nails. I cleared it. It felt exactly like winning gold to beat him at something.

The Olympics continued after supper, until Mother called us in for the night. We huddled in Dare's room, towels rolled around our necks like we'd seen athletes on TV do, making plans to open the Olympics to everyone in the neighborhood. He'd ride his bike one direction down the road to see if the Sawyer boys could come over, and I'd ride the other way to ask the kids who rode the school bus with us. The plan was to invite as many kids as we could find. We'd divide everyone into countries. Dare and me would be America. It was our yard, after all.

Dare strategized. "We'll make a point system and write down how many points each team gets. We might have to have one person be the official scorekeeper and add everything up. The team with the most points at the end will be the champions!"

"Should we make medals?" I considered the locket I had gotten for Christmas. Nobody could take it home, of course, but maybe the winners could wear it for a while. A dime fit perfectly in it. The small print shop down the road had a Coke machine on the porch, and if you put a dime in the slot an icy cold bottle of Coca-Cola would clunk out the bottom. If there weren't any people at the shop, no one minded if you sat on the porch steps and savored the whole bottle, leaving the empty in the wooden crate there. On days when there were customers, I'd make my way back down the road, hopping on the white lines that were cooler than the pavement, trying to keep the tar off my feet. The empty locket bounced light as sunshine on my chest.

"We'll make podiums, a high one and two lower ones, and the winners can stand on them and be saluted."

"Three winners?"

"First, second and third, mo-ron, just like the Olympics.

We're going to sweep it! We'll be the champions!"

I decided to ignore his stretched out 'mo-ron' since he wanted me on his team. I didn't brag out loud, but I could run and jump faster and farther than any of the girls and most of the boys in my class.

We won most of the games that we set up, and on days when nobody could come play, Dare and I would match up again. When fall came, we waited for the school bus, stomping our feet in the early morning chill. At the end of the driveway, we'd choose rocks the size of bluebird's eggs to throw over the telephone wires that looped down the road as far as the eye could see. He cleared the highest one almost every time; mine went somewhere into the middle wires. One winter later, I'd be able to hurl a stone over the highest wire, but by then things had changed. We had different games and Dare tossed rocks in an offhand manner without effort or thought. He would skim rocks on water the same way, haphazardly, without really noticing the rock or the water.

Everything was more fun as a contest—spitting, eating corn on the cob, even some chores. One Saturday in late fall, when it was time to carry firewood from the woods to the garage, we revived the log-carrying contest. The goal was to carry the most and the heaviest logs from the woods to the garage without stopping or dropping any along the way. Getting them piled up in your arms and still being able to see over them was the tricky part. There was a technique to loading—resting a couple of logs in the crook of the left arm while reaching down with the right to add more. A squat was more effective than a bend. Balance was key.

That day, I got four logs loaded in my arms, instead of my usual three, and could just see over the top by holding them a little lower than normal. Daddy's ax pounding into pine rounds echoed in my chest. Dare gave a whoop. "She's got four up!" he said in a sports announcer voice. "But can she get them to the garage?"

Daddy's ax didn't pause. Who knows whether he had even looked over in our direction? "Can she do it? Can she make it all the way?" Dare was still yelling like a sports broadcaster even though he was right beside me, falling into step with my unsteady course. He hadn't even bothered to carry any firewood. I sensed he was actually pulling for me and wouldn't try to trip me, since he had been managing four logs for a while. The obstacle that stopped me was one I never saw coming. Mother. As I gained the backyard, clearly on track to make a successful finish, her voice sliced out of the kitchen window.

"Wilhelmina Mae Miller!" Nothing good ever comes from the full name. A million thoughts flew through my head—Mrs. Gaylord called about the playground fight, but no, not on Saturday, she found the grass stains on my school clothes she'd warned me to change out of before playing, she—

"You drop them heavy logs right now!" She was standing on the back steps now, looking mad. "Right now, I said."

I dropped the logs. Dare began to fade back.

"Drop them and come in the house this instant."

I looked down at the already dropped logs, swallowed hard, and slowly walked toward the backdoor to find out what I'd done.

She went in ahead of me muttering loud enough for me to hear the disjointed phrases, " . . . no wonder half the time she thinks she's a boy . . . might as well be a field hand, fingernails dirty as sin, pine sap in her hair . . . Walter can just get Dare to help from now on. . . ."

The steady thud of the ax continued in the background. Dare was gone. I wondered what Daddy would think when I didn't come back for another load. I hoped he'd be mad and tell Mother I needed to get back out there. It wouldn't count if I didn't make it all the way to the garage, that's the rule. I had been so close.

"There's plenty for you to do inside the house," she was

saying, "and you can start by stripping the sheets off all the beds."

Inside work. I wanted to cry. I still didn't know what I had done to deserve this. After supper that night, I heard her talking to Daddy in the living room. She was talking in the voice she mainly used for us.

"She's not a boy! You seem to forget sometimes, she's a girl. . . ."

I wasn't sure what that had to do with carrying logs, but nobody seemed able to forget I was a girl after that. Even I couldn't seem to get it out of my head.

As it got closer to Christmas, Dare and I were both inside more. We spat orange seeds to see who could get them in the fireplace from farther away. We flicked the juice that rolled down our fingers at each other. The fire crackled into shades of orange, red, blue. He wanted a gun and so did I.

On Christmas morning, one of us got our wish. He got a shotgun and box of shells. I got a Betsy Wetsy, a tea set, and the usual amount of new clothes. On top of everything else, Dare and Daddy were going off to the woods to test out his shotgun. Mother was adamant—I wasn't going. Dare averted his eyes and wouldn't even join my cause. Mother relented only to the point that I could go outside in the backyard, but *not* to the woods. It was better than nothing, but not by much.

I stamped around in the yard with stinging eyes. All of my presents were inside toys. I kicked at the thin, lacy ice around some old puddles. I jumped on a branch that hadn't yet been cleared out of the yard, finding some satisfaction in the splintering sound of it breaking like frail bones.

Dare was so excited when he came back from the woods that he was babbling. "Man, this thing kicks! It's nothing like a BB gun. Ka-blam! I mean, it is loud. You heard it, right?" After a while he seemed to notice I hadn't said anything. He sprinted to the garage and came back still holding his shotgun but with his old Daisy BB gun in his other hand.

"Here. You can shoot this. Practice aiming with it." It was always a big deal when he let me shoot it, so I knew this was his way of making up for me not getting a gun for Christmas when he did. I knew it, but my throat felt too tight for talking.

"Look," he said. "Soon as I shoot something for real, I'll bring it back for you to see. You can watch me skin it."

I took the BB gun.

"Look," he started again, this time in a low whisper. "As soon as Daddy lets me go out on my own, we can meet by the old fort. I'll let you come with me."

Just then Daddy came back out, carrying his gun rags and oil.

"Got a couple more things to show you, son," he said, walking toward the garage. And Dare fell in behind him without even looking back.

I was left again. I pumped the arm of the old Daisy furiously. From beside the back steps I pulled a Coke bottle out of the wooden crate where they were stored until we took them back to the Winn Dixie for the deposit money. I set the bottle on the fence by the garden, stepping backwards and away from it in slow, steady paces. My throat still burned and my eyes felt raw. I shot at that hourglass shape until I was out of ammo. It was impervious to the tinging BBs. I wanted to blast it to smithereens. I dropped the gun and grabbed the bottle by the neck, smashing it against a half a brick that was edging the garden until it shattered and I got scared. I looked towards the house wondering if Mother had seen, but I knew she would be busy with Christmas dinner. I used one of the larger, sharper shards to scrape a small gash into the almost frozen ground where I buried the broken glass. *Bitch.* I said the cuss word out loud and felt my face get hot and my blood race.

I tore back to the house on that adrenaline, knowing I'd be expected to set the table before long, and I'd better wash my hands good before anyone saw or questioned how I'd gotten so dirty.

The Great Whore of Babylon

I had first settled the spot under the Nandina bush in the backyard when I still made mud pies and played with dolls. It was right under the kitchen table window where I could hear Mother's voice even though she was in the house and I was outside. Later, I loved it because it was great for eavesdropping. I could hear anything that was said in the kitchen where most of the talking got done on the phone or at the table. The summer that Aunt Etta came from Georgia to stay with us for a week, I camped there most days.

One of those nights, just as it was starting to get dark and the frogs were tuning up with their noise, I settled in to listen to Mother and Aunt Etta talk religion. Not the Sunday School *Jesus loves me this I know* kind. They focused on the scary stuff like the Rapture and the tribulation. They talked about the dark horses, the mark of the beast, the horrors that would happen as soon as Jesus got back to earth. Aunt Etta said in her preacher voice, "We're living in the last days." I knew some of the story, enough to make me get right with the Lord regularly after my panicked eavesdropping over the years. I sometimes wondered if there was a limit to how many times you could get saved before God just drew the line and said no more. Mother and Aunt Etta sat over endless coffee, previewing the second coming, weaving it together in the double stitching of their voices. They were saved. They had nothing to fear. They would fly up in the air with Jesus during the Rapture. Even so, when they talked about the end days, I could hear the low throb of terror pulsing through. They would shake their heads, picturing all those left behind people getting tortured.

"The time truly is at hand," Aunt Etta said.

"Truth is, I feel right sorry thinking about some folks going through the tribulation. Especially those people that just try to do good but ain't right with the Lord." Mother had her soft spots.

"Well, let him who has an ear hear!" Aunt Etta was the preacher of the family, sounded like she was behind a pulpit even when she was just talking about rain coming. When she and Mother fell into talking, Mother sounded even more country than usual.

Aunt Etta always wanted me and Dare to be 'witnesses for the Lord,' but I didn't have it in me. Most of the time I wasn't even saved, and I figured the Lord had plenty of people spreading the gospel. There were even big road signs up on the highway like the one that said **REPENT OR FACE ETERNAL DAMNATION**. I loved that sign because of the cuss word, but it still made me a little nervous when I looked at those bright red flames licking up from the bottom. Aunt Etta carried tracts in her pocketbook to hand out to people. I'd pretty much rather curl up and die than hand out tracts to folks I don't know.

" . . . The mountains will be cast into the sea . . . then the sea will turn to blood, and Wormwood will turn the waters bitter. . . ." As if on cue, Aunt Etta was reviewing how it was all going to happen.

This was the complicated part. I could never quite put together the whole story. I shut my eyes to listen better.

" . . . Woe to the inhabitants of the Earth in that day. There will be plagues of locusts, boils, frogs. . . ."

My eyes flew open to the deafening sound the frogs were making. But no. Not now. Mother and Aunt Etta wouldn't be sitting at the table drinking instant coffee with condensed milk if it were tonight. Besides, all the pictures of the Rapture I'd seen were in daytime.

"All the inhabitants of the earth will worship the beast."

"Except those whose names are written in the Book of Life," Mother chimed in, the security of being born again like gravy in her voice.

"When the hour of judgment is come, the Great Whore of Babylon will be cast down. Pastor Gray says she represents a place of sin and shame, just like the Bride of Christ represents a people."

"Like New York."

"Uhm hmmmm," Aunt Etta made that noise that meant *I don't want to point out to you that you're wrong.* She was younger than Mother, but she had gone to two years of junior college in Valdosta, and so was the most educated in the family. She also concentrated a lot of effort on studying the Bible, while Mother seemed to just like to read Psalms in the evening.

"Well if there's a place more full of sin and shame than New York, I'm sure I don't know it. Not that I've traveled all that much." She knew what Aunt Etta wasn't saying. When she was first married, Aunt Etta had taken a trip up to Staten Island. No one else in the family had ever stepped foot above the Maryland state line.

"Well. It may represent more than one place. Or it might not be *literally* a place at all. There's a lot of evil in the world, and a lot more to come." Aunt Etta had apparently decided to keep working together on the story. Sometimes they got off track and just argued about this or that, but tonight seemed like they were going to spin it out together.

"Amen to that. I pray no one I know is here to see the day when the Lord pours out his wrath upon the earth."

"When those trumpets sound and the earth and sky are rent, those who scorned his word and scorned those who tried to deliver it will rue the day. Hail and fire mixed with blood will rain down and the destruction of the earth will begin."

"The waters will run with blood," Mother emphasized in her amen voice.

"Imagine! Right off a third of the earth destroyed and the four horsemen loosed to roam, to torment and torture without end. Plagues, famine, people will wish they was dead. And irregardless of whoever or whatever the Great Whore of Babylon is, spending eternity in lakes of fire wouldn't be worth no amount of money or pleasure here on earth." Aunt Etta had taken the pulpit.

Suddenly, unexpectedly, Mother laughed. "You know Alma called Liz Taylor the Whore of Babylon. I swan, I thought I'd pee myself laughing. The way she carried on with that Richard Burton while they was both married! Alma brung over her magazines to show the pictures of them now that they're married, for her umpteenth time. She looked like a cat that got in the cream and the two of them talking about being in love like they invented it. How shamed you reckon her folks are?"

"For you have had five husbands, and the one you have now is not your husband!" Aunt Etta boomed as they both cracked up.

I wanted them to get back to the tribulation and what would happen next. They hadn't said the part about the 666 marked on everyone's forehead yet. I didn't like when they skipped around or went off on movie star tangents. It made it hard to get a handle on how everything was going to happen. I thought I had heard them talk about a dragon once, or maybe I'd fallen asleep while they were talking. That was a long time ago, and I couldn't picture how a dragon figured in. It sounded more like a fairy tale sort of thing, and I had begun to doubt its place in the end of times. It was part of the mystery that still needed to be cleared up.

" . . . You never know who she'll sink claws in next. . . ." They were just cracking themselves up and it was clear that Revelations was over for a while.

My foot had fallen asleep. I crawled out from my spot and stood there waiting for the pins and needles to go out of my foot. Mother stuck her head out the back door and yelled for me.

"I'm right here," I said, moving toward the pool of light she had flicked on at the back steps.

"Come on in. It's dark. Hurry and don't let the bugs in."

Already moths flitted around the outside light. Mother was just a shadow in the doorway.

"It's time for you to get a bath and go to bed."

I half ran, half hopped into the house, then to my room to grab my nightgown, wondering what it would be like if she turned on the faucet and blood came out instead of water. But then, she'd be gone already, and I'd come down to a blood bath all alone.

Jars

"... And clear that nasty jar of sludge off the steps before someone trips over it." Mother finished off whatever she had been saying with a command.

My corn flakes were already mushy so I took the bowl to the sink. Outside in the sunlight, the water in the jar did look like sludge—greenish-brown, with tadpoles floating like lopsided smiles. I knew enough to dump them away from the house, so I went out to the azalea bushes in the front yard.

Mother didn't care if we used old kitchen jars to catch things in, so long as we didn't use her good canning jars. With Dare's pocket knife, we'd punch holes in the lid so our captives could breathe. We didn't set out to kill them. Tadpoles, lightning bugs, caterpillars, ladybugs, we just wanted to watch them, or even better—see them transform.

I rinsed out the jar with the hose. Tadpoles disappointed us every year. I broke off a small branch from the azalea bush. It stood upright just perfectly in the jar, and the flower made a nice touch, a pink ceiling for my next guest. I pulled up some grass and clover and dropped it in. There had been a lot of caterpillars around lately, and wouldn't it be even better to see one of them spin itself into a cocoon and emerge as a butterfly than to see something grow into a frog? I left the jar under the azalea and went off towards the backyard. I had seen some just a day or so ago near the woods.

I went past the garden but stayed in the semi-cleared area on the edge of the woods. I looked in the leafy bushes and it didn't take long before I saw one making his way up a branch. I put my finger out in front of him and he climbed on, bunching up then stretching out his black and yellow bands along my finger and prickling onto my arm in slow, tickly movements.

I put my left pointer finger in front of him and he detoured onto it. As I watched him, I saw out of the corner of my eye other caterpillars on the bush. But I was happy with just this one. I carried him back to the front yard and he seemed content crawling up first one arm and then the other.

When I dropped him in his new home, he climbed onto the azalea twig just as I had pictured. I put some green leaves in for him to eat. I screwed the lid on and put him in the shade, but soon he had no more room to climb and he just stayed there at the top of the branch. He was more fun crawling up my arms, so I took him back out.

I thought he should have a name. Then it came to me: *Billy*, for Birdy's brother, a family name. It was silly to name or talk to a caterpillar, but no one was around.

"Hey, Billy," I said as he started his route up my arm. "You're my first pet caterpillar. You'll be a butterfly one of these days if you don't die." Billy waggled his antennae as if agreeing.

That night after supper, I went out to check on Billy. He raised his head, antennae moving, like he was trying to look at me, too. I thought of the way he felt on my arm, the little tickle of his travel. I thought I knew what he was trying to say, so I unscrewed the lid. I left it beside the jar where he was still clinging to the twig.

Whenever I saw a yellow and black butterfly that summer, I thought *that could be him, our Billy.*

Winning Prisoner

Of the indoor games we played, Prisoner was one of Dare's favorites. One day after supper, when I had been tied to the small ladder back chair in Dare's room for what felt like hours, it became my least favorite. The light had leached away leaving me in a gathering dusk. At least he hadn't blindfolded me, though he had gagged me and it was causing my jaw to ache. I squirmed more and tried to loosen the various cords holding my hands behind the chair. My wrists were chafed and my armpits and shoulders throbbed from the slung back position. *I hate this game*, I thought, in a red fury. Dare always got out of my knots in a matter of minutes, no matter how tight I pulled or how many times I tripled them. *I never win this game. Never.* I could hear the muffled sound of TV voices coming from the living room and knew he was in there watching some show while I was still tied up, now on the verge of tears. *I hate him*, I thought, imagining him watching television while I was about to be sitting alone in the dark. I made muffled gagging sounds in my attempts to scream but knew, even as I tried, that he'd never hear over the TV. I'd already tried stomping the chair around, but it only hurt my armpits more. I was in his room, so no one would think to look for me there. But then, he'd have to go to bed sometime, and so would I, and then Mother would ask where I was. I tried to resign myself.

Looking around the small room, I remembered why there were two twin beds in here. Granddaddy had slept in one. I was only little then, but I remembered him. I remembered his rough, stubbly cheek when he would put me to bed or lift me out. He was a gray man—gray hair, gray cheek stubble, even his skin seemed grayish. He sang songs to us and gave us candy. We used to raid his possessions hunting for hidden candy, digging into the deep pockets of his overcoat, going through his medicine chest. Sometimes we found it, lint-flecked marshmallow peanuts dredged from his bathrobe or old Tootsie Rolls in the pocket of his trousers. Most of the time, we had to wait for him to decide when we'd been good enough to be given some. I knew he had died, but I couldn't remember how. It had to be while he was living here in Dare's room. I tried to think of what had happened and I wished Dare would come in and untie me because he would know. Not to mention, I was sick of this dumb game and I would never ever play it again. My arms really, really hurt, but a shadow was starting to take shape. We were sitting at the table, but not eating, and Daddy was telling us about heaven. He was telling us Granddaddy had gone there. I remembered now. I had been paying more attention to Dare because he was biting his lip like he did when he was trying hard not to cry, and I was wondering why he was almost crying and whether he was in trouble. But then Mother started to cry and blew her nose in a handkerchief, and just about then Dare broke down. I started crying, too, because everyone else was, and I just couldn't help it. What Daddy had been saying was Granddaddy was dead. Why hadn't I remembered that before? I must have noticed he didn't lift me out of bed anymore or say prayers with me. I tried to think of what happened. I couldn't remember ever going to a funeral for him. It was like there was this blank screen in my head. I looked around the room and I could re-furnish it with his stuff. He had half the dresser top, and on his side was a comb, a razor, a framed family picture of him and his wife and their kids, and one of those kids was my mother. He would hold it up for me as he rested me on a hip, point her out, and say something like that I was the spittin' image of her. We had done this many times. I'd ask to see that picture of when Mother was little, and he'd bring me in and show me. He smelled like Aqua Velva. He always wore long-sleeved shirts. I heard Mother one day explain to a neighbor lady why he'd wear long sleeves even in the dog days of summer. She said he had gotten a tattoo in his young days, but once he was born again he was embarrassed about it. I thought about Uncle Erskine's tattoo and wondered whether Granddaddy also had a bare-naked mermaid on his arm. I started to feel bad about how I'd forgotten about him, and about how much I couldn't remember still. Had I even seen his tattoo ever? What was that song he used to sing when he was getting me to fall asleep? . . . *I see the moon and the moon sees me, down through the leaves of the old oak tree.* That was one of them. Folks still sing that to kids. He had half the closet, too. I could only remember that big black overcoat, though, because of the candy. Heavy, wool. I could hear him and Dare sometimes talking in their room at night when I was in bed. I started to feel scared then. The room was completely dark. I wanted to cry. What if other people die—would I just keep going along as if nothing happened, as if they had just been visiting? Where was I when Granddaddy was buried? *I don't even know where his grave is,* I thought miserably. And then I did start to cry. It started to feel like everyone was gone and I was just tied to a chair for no good reason and I would die there, too. Then I heard Dare turning the door handle, and a slice of light came in from the hall. He stood there laughing, which made me cry harder, and I started feeling like I was choking. He came around and untied my feet, then hands, but waited a long, mean minute before he undid the gag.

"I hate you," I spat, wiping my face with my shirt.

"Same to ya."

"I've been in here for hours."

"You're such a crybaby. You've been in here maybe one hour tops."

"I saw Granddaddy." A sudden panic shot through me. Where had that come from? Why did I say that?

Dare flicked on the light and stared at me. "What did you say?"

"I saw Granddaddy."

"Liar!"

If I had been planning to back out of the lie somehow, I knew now it was impossible. "He was wearing a long-sleeved plaid shirt all buttoned up even though it's hot in here."

"I don't believe you."

"He was looking for you, to tell you to stop messing with me." It was coming back, the way he would say *Don't momick your little sister like that, son. You're her older brother—you got to look after her.* I could almost really hear him say it. I could almost smell Aqua Velva. "The whole room smelled like Aqua Velva when he was here."

Dare sat down hard on the bed. He just stared at me like he was looking right through me. Then he sort of shook his head a little, clenched his jaw and said, "You're making it up."

Rubbing my sore wrists and getting up from the chair, I said, "He said he was sorry he didn't have candy. He couldn't bring it with him from where he was." I saw with alarm that Dare was biting his lip. Granddaddy and Dare had been real close, everybody knew it, but it was another thing I hadn't spent much time thinking about. I understood, with a mix of panic and triumph, that I'd shaken him, that he still hurt about Granddaddy dying. A few minutes ago, I hated him and would have done anything to hurt him, but now I felt a little scared and I also felt like I was missing something inside. Why didn't I want to cry over Granddaddy? It made me more curious than sad to think about his dying. Was I heartless? That was it! He had had a heart attack. I couldn't remember how I knew, but I did. And all those medicines, they were his 'heart pills.'

I took a few steps toward the door, but Dare wasn't looking at me. Then, out of nowhere, I turned around and said, "He was holding his heart. He told me it hurt his heart to see me all tied up like that."

Dare blinked hard about six times and stared at me like I was the ghost. Sounding like a frog croaking he said, "Get out. Get out of our room. I ain't playing with you, Willie." He got up like he might smack me. But he stopped and stood completely still. He had said *our* room, and I knew he was sharing it again with Granddaddy in his head. I was at the door in a blink, but before I closed it behind me I hissed through the crack, "I ain't playing that dumb game ever again."

When I got to my room I didn't even turn the light on. I sat on the edge of my bed looking out the window, thinking about what I'd done. It was mean, but so was Dare. Served him right. He thought he was so tough, but he was probably in there crying like a baby. Then I felt a stabbing in my center. Why wasn't I that upset thinking about Granddaddy? Didn't I love him, too? How could Dare, mean as he was, love somebody more than I did? I even had more leeway to cry since I was a girl, but here I was—completely dry-eyed—just wondering about details like what did that tattoo look like. I started humming . . . *and the moon sees me, down through the leaves of the old oak tree, please let the light that shines on me, shine on the one I love.* That made me feel a little teary, but I was still having to work at it. I thought of Dare in his room and I knew he was face down in the pillow, stifling himself so no one would hear him. And from some icy, dark place a knot slipped and I thought—with pure cold meanness—*I win.*

Rapture

The angle of light told me it was late morning. I stretched out and stared at dust motes drifting in the slatted light that sifted through the blinds. I hadn't heard Mother in the kitchen or Dare slamming around. I lazed, imagining the motes could swirl together into Tinkerbell or Glinda, some magical being alighting in my room, come to transport me. I wished I could fly. Not inside a house like Dorothy's dark ride, though—all on my own, lifting skyward. I drew my knees up, kicking off the sheet. The room was getting too stuffy to stay in much longer. The bars of sunlight across the bed were getting hot and if Mother had already poured milk into a cereal bowl for me, it would be getting warm, too. I sat up and raised the blinds from my perch on the bed. It was so quiet that it surprised me. I listened intently for a minute before hopping off the bed.

I splashed water and wet my toothbrush before going into the kitchen. No one was there. No bowl of milk either. No mother doing dishes at the sink. I felt a little uneasy stitch in my chest. Climbing on the counter to get a bowl, I made sure to make noise, clunk bowls, and slam the cabinet door. Nothing. I opened the refrigerator door and let the cool air wash over me. I held it open for a long time. I poured the cornflakes first instead of the milk, just the way I wasn't supposed to because of the splatter. I mashed the cornflakes into a milky mush, but no one came into the kitchen. A thread tightened through me. Scary words like *the rapture* and *the second coming* stitched their syllables in half thoughts and vague images. I had pondered these things just like I had thought about hell. Bad people splashing in lakes of fire, screaming, while above them good people drifted by on clouds, not smoke, just cool breezy clouds. The thread pulled taut and pulsed into needling heartbeats. The rapture: one day half the world would be gone, the good half. Some ordinary day you'd be walking along, or just waking up, and poof—a gazillion people disappear. That's how they said it would be. Just like that. A wink of an eye.

Then I got quiet, too. I walked very carefully to the front door. Open. Only the screen door was shut, but it was unlatched. I went out, stood on the first step, and called out, "Mother." Nothing. "Muuuuuther!" Nothing. No one whistling for a dog, no tractor in the field. A million thoughts whirled around—the long days of punishment, three sixes on my forehead, the Devil walking around right here on earth. I looked up at the thought of the saved bodies ascending but the sun was so bright it brought tears to my eyes. I ran around the side yard to the back, all the way back to the toolshed and stared at the garden, nobody. This was it. I had been left behind. I hadn't been saved for a long time. Probably since Vacation Bible School last summer, and I sort of cheated then. The world had never before been this quiet ever. I could hear my own heart beating. Then I began crying for real. Gulping in tears and snot and finally screaming, "MOTHER!" And there in the bean rows, half of Mother appeared. She rose and brought a hand to the top of her brow, squinting toward me. The thread snapped and a wash of relief, a welcome baptism, flooded me. I could have fallen right down in a prayer of rejoicing, but I just stood there, sniffling.

"Girl, what you doing out here in your nightie?" Mother called. "Get on in the house and put some clothes on, then come help me pick these string beans."

A choir of angels sang through the trees. I had been saved from the rapture. I wasn't left behind. I wasn't going to get tortured or burned. Not today, anyway. In my head, I said a quick prayer—*Thank you Jesus, Thank you Lord*—making a mental note to pray more later just in case.

"Yes, ma'am," I yelled back too loud so that Mother straightened up again to look at me. She shook her head before she bent back into the bean rows.

I Come to the Garden Alone

Half the kids being dropped off didn't even show up regular for Sunday School. Older kids had summer jobs, most of them in the fields. Some of the younger farm kids probably liked Vacation Bible School—they got to see other kids their age, drink a soda with their baloney sandwich, and get a bag of chips. Depending on how collections had gone at church there might be Nu-Grape, chocolate or orange soda in the ice tubs.

I knew my way around the church and went straight to room C for six-to-twelve-year-old Crusaders. The chairs were drawn into a circle. I claimed the one nearest the door. When we filed out for food and drinks, I wanted to be at the head of the line; the chocolate sodas, if they had them, would go fast. Our teacher, Miss Jean, herded in a bunch of kids who hadn't known where to go.

"Starting this morning, we are going to learn a Bible verse every day," Miss Jean piped. Her voice moved up and down in a musical way so that even though she refused to call me anything other than my full name, Wilhelmina Mae, it didn't sound as awful as it usually did. Miss Jean played piano most Sundays. "I want you to keep practicing because on Sunday your whole group will recite your verses in unison, that means all together." She beamed at us. I'd been learning scripture ever since I could remember. I didn't belong with this group of dum-dums. "Now some will be pretty long, so you'll have to practice at home. But today we'll start with an easy one that I hope you've heard before and some of you may already know it. If not, you'll know it by the end of the day because we're going to say it over and over so that it stays in your memory. How many of you know Psalm 23?" About half the class raised their hands. I could barely keep from rolling my eyes.

By the time we had read it over and said it out loud together three times, I was so crazy bored that I wanted to kick someone. Miss Jean wanted us to say all the words "in unison" as she kept saying, "clearly" and "all at the same time." I looked around and saw how hopeless this was and wondered why Miss Jean couldn't see it. Some of these kids talked like they had mouths stuffed with cotton. The stinky boy sitting next to me couldn't say his S's right. His crew cut was so short you could see his pink scalp, and I tried to move my chair a little in case he sprayed any spit with those S's. The kid on the other side wasn't much better. She was one of the youngest in the room, if size was any measure, and she kept slipping her hand up to her face and pulling it back down. I didn't know whether she meant to pick her nose or suck her thumb, but she looked so much like a baby that either seemed likely. Miss Jean could try until she was blue in the face, but they were just going to keep mumbling all those words into one big mush.

"Now, one more time. Only this time, see if you can follow my voice and say the words the same way as me. I'm going enunciate so everyone can hear, and then as soon as I stop, I want you to say what I just said, exactly the same way." Miss Jean walked around our circle, reciting Psalm 23 like she was singing it.

"The Lord is my shepherd; I shall not want," she chimed.

"The Lord is my shepherd; I shall not want." The ragtag echo sounded like a choir of drunks.

"He maketh me to lie down in green pastures."

They had an awful time with "maketh." The boy next to me said something like *green pathurth* after everyone else had already finished.

I wanted to scream.

Most of VBS was torture, beginning with having to wear shoes and sit inside all day. Then there was the tediousness of the lessons, but this reciting business was the worst.

They were starting at the top again, with *the Lord is my shepherd I shall not want,* when it flashed through me. *The Lord is my shepherd I shall not want.* It was like someone smacked me in the head. How had I missed that all these years? Is David really saying he doesn't want the Lord? I was stiff with shock. I looked at the piece of paper Miss Jean had passed around. There it was, plain as day.

> **The Lord is my shepherd; I shall not want.**
> **He maketh me to lie down in green pastures;**
> **he leadeth me beside the still waters.**
> **He restoreth my soul:**
> **he leadeth me in the paths of righteousness for his name's sake.**
> **Yea, though I walk through the valley of the shadow of death,**
> **I will fear no evil: for thou art with me;**
> **thy rod and thy staff they comfort me.**
> **Thou preparest a table before me in the presence of mine enemies:**
> **thou anointest my head with oil;**
> **my cup runneth over.**
> **Surely goodness and mercy shall follow me all the days of my life**
> **and I will dwell in the house of the Lord forever.**

David didn't *want* the Lord to be his shepherd, probably didn't want to lie down either. Even though some of it softened a little, like walking by still waters, I saw how much of this was something no one would want to do, like eating with your enemies. I knew all too well the rod was about getting a whipping—spare the rod and spoil the child. Bees buzzed in my head. I'd known these words my whole life, but I'd never realized just what they were saying.

Half the time I didn't care that I was a sinner, but I kept it secret. And here was a secret hiding in plain view—even David the Giant Slayer didn't want to be a Christian. My whole body hummed with this sudden knowledge. God had finally spoken to me. I knew being saved was still going to win out, though, because there was that matter of heaven or hell. It was like school, no one wanted to go, but no one wanted to be dumb either. But at least now, we faced each other a little more squarely. It was a little clearer where we stood, God and me.

Church Ladies

Miss Violetta was one of the church ladies who helped at every church social, prepared Christmas baskets every year, and taught at Vacation Bible School. She was famous for being the cleanest woman in the world, or in our world at least. My mother sometimes said, "Violetta's house is so clean you could eat dinner off the floor." I loved to just picture that: Mother squatting to daintily pick a drumstick off the floor, saying how delicious it is and what a fine cook Violetta is, while Miss Violetta unloads a quivering jello mold onto the linoleum and softly demurs.

Sometimes when Mother visited Miss Violetta's she'd bring me along. I don't think she had any kids of her own. There was no evidence of them, no pictures of any in her dim living room, none that I could see when I poked my head into bedroom doorways down the hallway to the bathroom. Even so, she had a swing set in her back yard that I could play on. There had been a husband, as wedding pictures and other framed photos around her house testified. I had learned from eavesdropping on the ladies' talk that he had been a sinner, never once came into church even though he brought her there, dropped her off, then would come back and wait in the parking lot until services were over to pick her up. He died. I always wondered whether he got right with the Lord beforehand. He must have, since otherwise he'd be in hell and Miss Violetta would never be able to get over that.

There was something more interesting than a sinner husband about Miss Violetta, though, and the other ladies talked in low voices about it now and then. They whispered into the phone or murmured over coffee, but no one said anything directly to her about it. The ladies never looked at her legs openly, only when they were walking behind her. Her legs were hairy. Not just a little bit, either. She had long black hairs on her legs that curled under her nylons. On Sundays, she'd come to church, always wearing a hat and gloves, trim and neat in her dresses, but with long black hairs pressed visibly under her stockings.

The ladies would speculate over afternoon coffee and pound cake.

"She is, in all other ways, so clean and neat. Why do you suppose. . . ?"

"Are her people foreigners? I've heard some of them don't shave their legs, armpits neither, if you can imagine that!"

"It's a shame, that's what it is. Why, she still has a waist, and she's neat as a pin. She takes good care of herself. Except for, well except for *that*."

These conversations always ended with a pitying shake of the head and a smug downward glance at smooth, crossed legs. Kids loved Miss Violetta. She was gentle and always had mints or chewing gum in her purse. She would stroke our hair and let us sit on her lap. She never said *now get on outside and play*. She never raised her voice.

Sometimes Mother let me sit with Miss Violetta during Sunday service. When we would bow our heads for a moment of prayer, I would keep my eyes open a slit and stare down at the long black hairs, pulled up, slightly curled, compressed tightly under a smooth stretch of nylon. I wanted to run my fingers along the thick webbing and trace out the secret of her hairy legs. Her ankles were small. And her feet looked at home in the pointy toed high heels, not stuffed in like sausages the way some of the ladies' feet looked. I liked sitting next to her because before we settled down for the long sermon, Miss Violetta would reach into her patent leather purse for a mint or piece of gum and give it to me. A red Life Saver could really help dull the pain of the preaching.

Sundays were a gamble, though. Church in summertime was pretty miserable no matter what. The windows open, the sills yellow with pollen, my crinoline slip embedding in my legs no matter how I sat. The women waved the air with cardboard fans. The pianist plunked mercilessly at "Onward Christian Soldiers" and "On the Wings of a Dove." The entire congregation would fall into a heat-drowsed stupor. Old Mr. Cartwright would start to snore and his daughter would elbow him in the ribs while trying not to wake up the baby she was holding in her arms.

The best Sundays were when the Holy Ghost came and everyone woke up. The air turned electric. The preaching shut down and the fun began. Sometimes Mr. Smithfield got the spirit and sprinted up and down the aisles, waving his arms and crying out "Hallelujah! Hallelujah!" or Miss Mabel Barker talked in tongues loud enough for the Methodists a mile down the road to hear. Then I'd quit playing tic-tac-toe on my knee and start paying attention. Another good Sunday was when a healing service was held. A healer would come every now and then, and people who had ailments could be delivered of them. The same people tended to get healed each time, often of the same complaint, but the show and sweat of it was as good as watching TV. Some healers pressed the ladies on the forehead until they fainted right down and had to be caught. I could just picture their sickness flying out the window, leaving them wobbly and off balance.

Once, Mother got healed. She had backaches a lot. The healer said that one of her legs was shorter than the other and this caused the backaches, so he pulled her short leg out. That whole week I begged her to let me measure her legs. She got so mad that I had to memorize extra scripture verses that week, more than we were assigned for Sunday School.

There was one Sunday service that caused talk for months on end. We were singing "When the Roll is Called up Yonder" when the spirit fell. People started praying out loud, hands waving, folks talking in tongues, everything. I watched Mr. Smithfield, making bets with myself about how long it would take before he made a break for the aisle. He rolled up onto the balls of his feet, up and back, up and back, faster and faster. Then he did it. He tore down the aisle with his eyes closed, never grazing a person, a pew, or anything solid, tangible. It was like he had radar, like bats at twilight.

I was sitting by Miss Violetta who was speaking softly in tongues with her eyes closed. Miss Mabel was sitting in front of us also speaking in tongues, getting louder and louder. I was watching her as she swayed and lifted both hands in the air. Mr. Smithfield was actually doing laps around the pews on the left side of the church. Straight out of nowhere, Miss Mabel sprang into the center aisle, almost at a dash, towards the pulpit. I was fixed on her because I had never seen her move like that. I thought she might join Mr. Smithfield's holy race she was moving so fast, but at the last row before the altar she caught the edge of the pew with her hip. I winced, knowing that must have hurt like the devil. She went down with one high heel scraping, as if to break the fall. Mr. Smithfield ran right up and stopped inches from her, staring down at her crumpled form. Then there was a fast blur of action. Mr. Smithfield and others were lifting her; she was shaking and crying. I had moved all the way over to the edge of the pew, gawking. Her high heel had carved a long pale gash into the wood floor. They carried her out the door. Miss Violetta leaned over, scooped up the purse Miss Mabel had left on the pew, and sailed out the door behind them, seeming to move on air. When she returned, she patted my hand and smiled at me like I was the one who had been hurt, then reached for her own purse. Bonus round Life Saver. I scooted over closer to her and she put her arm on the pew behind me in a protective sort of way. I could hear a car spraying gravel out of the parking lot. Later I found out that Mrs. Cook, the preacher's wife, drove Miss Mabel to the hospital where an X-ray revealed a fractured hip.

In our car on the way home, me and Dare couldn't stop from whispering about it. From where Dare had been sitting, on the other side of the church with the Pearl family who had boys his age, it looked like Mr. Smithfield had knocked her down. I told him how it really happened, but Mother told both of us to shush. I was sorry she had been hurt; still, this had to have been one of the best Sundays ever.

Throughout the rest of that summer and other summers that piled up year after year, when the preacher's voice droned across the stuffy room, my eyes would seek out the white scratch from Miss Mabel's shoe. It grew so thin and covered over that eventually, I was just looking at a place, like any other, on the floor. But I knew the mark was there, a testament to an act of faith—or of folly—that no one talked about anymore, etched in wood, filled in grain by grain, until it became invisible.

Nighttime Stories

The heat becomes a monster. It's bad in the daytime but you can turn on the garden hose and spray yourself, or go to the woods where it's cooler. At night it seems worse, so muggy hot that even a thin sheet feels like too much covers for your sticky skin. The fans set in the windows turned up high to blow in enough night air to cool the hot, stuffy rooms sometimes just blow humid air from one place to another. Still, some breeze feels better than no breeze. This was one of those nights when I couldn't sleep and the fan whirred almost uselessly. I heard Mother coming down the hall toward my room. Sometimes you just know what's about to happen, and in that way, I knew she was coming to turn the fan off so it wouldn't run all night, wasting electricity. She peeked her head in the doorway.

"It's too hot," I said to let her know I was awake and to not turn off the fan yet.

"You're a night owl, Willie. You ought to be in dreamland by now."

Sounded like she was in a soft mood, so I sat up a little.

"Will you tell me a story?"

"Oh Lord, girl. It's late. I'm wore out. Did you say your prayers?"

"Yes ma'am. Just a short little story?"

She came over and sat on the edge of my bed. She brushed my damp bangs off my forehead and sighed. "I don't have any stories this evening. I'm ready for bed myself."

"What's a joot joint?"

"A what? Where did you hear that?"

"Birdy said her brother that died went to a joot joint. I think he might have been in a car accident."

"Birdy tole you that?"

"She told me he went to a joot joint and I figured out the car accident part myself."

"You did, did you?" Her voice was teasing, but not mean.

"She don't like to talk about it, but she told me he rode out to a joot joint and then he died, so I figured he must have been in a crash. Was he?"

"Juke joint."

"Huh?"

"It's not 'joot' joint, it's 'juke' joint."

"Oh. What is that anyway?"

"A dancehall sort of place."

I thought about that for a minute. Mother and Daddy didn't dance; no one in our church did. It's not exactly a sin, at least not one that gets preached about, but if you're saved you just don't. Billy loved to dance. It's what they always say about him when I ask. I felt a flicker of worry in case he wasn't saved. He was still a kid when he died, or at least not yet grown up.

"How old was he, Birdy's brother, when he died? Did Daddy know him?"

"He died long before your daddy was born, Willie." Her voice wasn't smiling anymore. "I don't know his exact age, but he hadn't graduated yet, though to hear Birdy speak of it, he all but had a Harvard diploma in his hand."

"A what?"

"Nothing. You go to sleep now." She stood up and then bent to kiss me where she'd brushed my bangs back.

"I thought you was going to tell me about the car accident?"

Mother snorted. "Well, I don't know nothing about a car accident your great uncle Billy might or might not have been in. He's been dead long enough to have been turned to gold. Whatever he was really like, and what happened that night out there on Old County Road, folks may never know, or at least not remember."

So. Mother knew something. It was clear by the way she said it that she and Birdy didn't see eye to eye on the dead boy.

There was more than one big gap between the way Mother and Birdy saw things.

"Birdy said everybody loved Billy."

"I suppose everyone Birdy knew did love Billy. But Billy probably knew a few more people than the Willoughby family and their silver spoon set. He weren't at no country club the night he ended up dead, that's for sure."

"What was the name of that place?"

"I have no idea, Willa Mae. I have never in my life set foot in one of them places and don't plan to. You ask a lot of silly questions for a girl that ought to be asleep."

"If someone would just tell me, I wouldn't keep asking."

For some reason, Mother sat back down then. She just sat there, staring in the dark, until I thought there might be something wrong.

Then she said, "Willie, you cain't keep poking around in people's business like you do. But you're right about not knowing and how that makes you overly curious. I'll tell you what, Billy would have been your daddy's uncle, and even your own daddy don't know what all happened to him. So, it's not like we've been keeping some big secret from you. Whatever it was, it wasn't like he was a war hero or something, so just take all that *Billy was God's gift to the world* talk with a grain of salt. He had been out to a place where people drink, smoke, cuss, gamble, dance, and Lord only knows what else. Lot of no-count folks end up in those places and sometimes bad things happen, fights and such. Different kind of folks go there, and I reckon it's some high society folks' idea of fun to rub shoulders with migrant field hands and other riff raff. I don't know how many times Billy woulda been out there, but one night he didn't come back alive. Maybe it was cause his car landed in the ditch, but it seems doubtful that's what killed him. More likely he got in a fight with somebody who pulled a knife. Now that ought to be enough to give you nightmares. I must be addled myself to be telling you all this when you ought to be asleep already." But she stayed sitting on the bed.

"I don't get nightmares. I don't mean to be nosy but I ought to know about my own family, right? It's not being a busybody when it's your own kin, is it?"

"No. I reckon not. But now you know as much as I do about it, and that's enough. This isn't something you need to be talking about with anyone else, not even Birdy. Especially not Birdy. And no one outside the family neither."

"I know. I'm not dumb."

"No, Willie, you ain't dumb. But you know what they say, curiosity killed the cat."

"But satisfaction brought him back."

Mother laughed. I felt starry with pleasure.

"You got a quick tongue. I hope it don't get you in as much trouble as it's likely to. Now get to sleep."

She left the fan on, pausing in the doorway. For a soaring moment, I thought she might say something else, maybe add to the Billy story, but she didn't. Her heavy-heeled footsteps went around the house as she turned out lights, then disappeared into the dark of her and Daddy's room.

I lay there mulling over the new details. I started erasing the car smash-up that I'd been picturing and felt almost giddy with the even worse thing: it could have been a knife fight. Mother had pretty much said that Billy wasn't as perfect as Birdy made him out to be. She had said it in the same sort of voice she used talking to the church ladies. I couldn't for the life of me remember a time when she'd just flat-out told me something about the grown-up world. I felt bigger than my own body and hoped she'd keep talking to me like that instead of always trying to shoo me away from the grown-ups. But for now, I really just needed to think about this new piece a little more. I needed to see how that golden boy, who wore a ridiculous velvet suit with a lace collar in his baby picture, grew up to be someone who could get in a knife fight and be killed. It was almost too good to be true.

In Trouble

I could hear Mother's voice on the phone as I made my sleepy way down the hall towards the kitchen.

"I swan, Violetta, you are not going to believe what I found out today! Alma's oldest son has gone and gotten some girl in trouble."

Her back was to me as she cradled the receiver between her ear and shoulder, leaving her hands free to dip into the sink full of just washed strawberries. She capped and sliced each one into a big bowl. This sounded good. Someone was in trouble and it wasn't me. I rubbed my eyes and tiptoed over to the spot on the other side of the refrigerator where Mother couldn't see me. I slunk down to my usual eavesdropping position, chin on knees, not making a sound.

"I don't know. Some Tidewater girl spending the summer with her kinfolk down the lane from Alma's. I don't know 'em or what congregation they belong to. I know Alma raised her boys right, though."

I wished I could hear what Miss Violetta was saying, too. I waited.

"Well, what do you think? There'll probably be a hurry-up wedding. I know Alma'll make sure they do the right thing by her."

"Mmmhmm. Ricky was always the good one, too. It was Ronnie was always getting into trouble. But this . . . well this must just be breaking Alma's heart."

Mother stood there listening and then laughed in a short burst.

"Well, you know first babies have a habit of coming early. Wouldn't do to count how many in our congregation alone. Vera told me, and she had it straight from Alma herself, a complete surprise. Didn't know Ricky had even talked to the girl. I heard she's in her last year of high school so that's good, considering what happened with poor Percy Lamb."

I was starting to get hungry. I could smell the strawberries she was slicing and wished I could put some in a bowl with some milk and cereal, but if she saw me she'd change the subject until I was out of the kitchen. I didn't know Percy Lamb, but Miss Alma's two boys went to our church. I wanted to know what Ricky had done to get in trouble.

"You don't remember that? Oh lordy, I thought the Lambs would just die of shame after he got that girl in trouble. Her people were some sort of country club set, and since she wasn't quite turned 15 yet they charged him with statutory. It was the biggest mess. Can you even imagine?" She made her disapproving humming noise. "I don't know what they was thinking. People turned against her instead. Bringing the law into it like that. Like it's not a private matter. Everyone knew Percy wouldn't hurt a fly, much less force a girl. They was all over each other right out in plain view. It was clear as the nose on my face what was going on there, but her people acted like she was innocent as the day she was born and Percy ruined her."

I wondered if she planned to make strawberry shortcakes. I hoped so.

"No ma'am, they did not. Her parents took her on vacation and they came back without it."

Whenever Mother made strawberry shortcakes there would either be ice cream or whipped cream to go on it. My stomach rumbled at the thought.

"No, I kid you not, that's exactly what they did."

I thought about last night, how she'd told me that Billy wasn't as perfect as Birdy always said he was. It made sense, everybody gets in trouble at some point. It was almost like Birdy was protective of him even though he died so long ago.

"Ain't that the truth! Bad enough they didn't keep a better eye on her, but then to go and do that. And that was after they'd made a public display of themselves bringing the law against Percy like it was all his fault and none theirs. Last I heard, they had moved someplace up north. One of them peculiar places. Rhode Island, maybe."

They were still talking about Percy, whoever he was. I wished they'd get back to Ricky.

"Mmmhmm. Probably scarred for life. And what decent fellow is going to want to get mixed up with someone like that? Course, it ain't entirely her fault. I put more fault on her mama and daddy. What kind of people would be willing to do that to their own flesh and blood, no matter how it came?"

Mother was nodding with the phone still crooked between her hitched up shoulder and her ear. She must be getting a neck crick by now.

"That's the Lord's truth, ain't it? People will accept an early baby. But decent folk sure ain't going to accept *that*." She paused. "Oh Lord no. He married that Templeton gal a couple of years back and to my knowledge they don't even have any young'uns. He's done good despite all that mess."

An early baby. I suddenly got it. Some girl Ricky had been talking to was going to have a baby before she was married. He was going to have to marry her. She was 'in trouble' because she was having a baby. He was the one that got her in trouble. I wasn't clear on all the details, but I'd heard about girls getting in trouble before.

"I don't rightly remember what happened with the law. I know he didn't get sent off or nothing like that. His family had a hard time of it, though. Can you imagine having your son accused of that? And it wasn't like they could just pick up and move off somewhere. The Lambs have lived on that farm for as long as anyone can remember. But they sure ain't living high off the hog."

She listened to what Miss Violetta was saying and I wished again that I could hear, too.

"Well, they say every cloud's got a silver lining and I guess Alma can count that as one. I don't know who that Tidewater girl is, but looks like her family ain't crazy enough to try to pull something like that. They all sat down at Alma's to work it out, must be good folks even if the girl don't know enough to keep her knees together."

I pulled my chin off my knees and looked at them. Mother had some country sayings that were a puzzle. Ricky Sawyer was in high school. I wondered where he and the girl would live when they got married. I wondered whether she would just move into Miss Alma's house and stay in Ricky's room. It was strange to think of him being married, and then a daddy, too. He worked in the lumber mill during the summer. Maybe he'd work there all year now.

"Well that's what I'm saying. Ricky hisself might a been a little on the early side. And I don't mean anything by that either. Willa Mae was early, too, but thank heavens she was a second child, not a first, or just imagine what people might a thought."

I was an early baby? That didn't sound good. Sounds like I started out on the wrong foot.

"I reckon she could use our prayers right now. And of course, don't breathe a word about this to anyone."

Mother was finished with the strawberries and it was now or never to grab some before she put them away. I got up and moved back closer to the hallway and then yawned loud like I was just walking in.

"Violetta? My sleepyhead just got up and I 'spect I'd better get to the garden before it gets too hot out there."

They had begun the long process of saying goodbye, and I had a cereal bowl full of strawberries. The cornflakes were still on the table from Dare's breakfast. I poured milk without splashing and started crunching away. I hoped the Tidewater girl would be in church on Sunday with the Sawyer family so I could get a good long look at her.

Fire Bug

Dare was off again, who knows where. Maybe he rode his bike to Feral or went fishing. I was beginning to wonder whether he would ever include me again. This was the most boring summer in the history of summers. I wandered past the garden toward the woods. The smell of sunbaked pine needles filled the air. I followed the path straight through the woods, right up to where Mr. Sample's woods and small back fields began. The tractor ruts behind his barn had dried into hard ridges and minnow puddles were scarce now. I sat down inside the bowl of two large roots that circled above ground, under the tree that had three sets of initials carved into it. Daddy's initials were deep, and cracks had spread from them across the bark. Dare's initials were newer and not yet cracked. Mine were under Dare's and shallow in comparison. I had stolen Dare's pocket knife and hidden it here in the circle of roots to work on that. Instead, I held the knife by its tip, then threw it at a pine in front of me, but the knife just glanced off and fell to the ground. I didn't feel like getting up to get it. Flies whirred. Birds competed, bobwhites repeating in the background, robins all around, blue jays scrapping over something in their mean, shrill way. I thought back to last summer when Dare taught me to smoke using hollow reeds that we could break into cigarette-sized stalks. I could do it without him, though. I got up, grabbed the knife, folded it closed, and ran back through the woods to the garden shed to see if there were still some matches in the rusty coffee can. And there they were, not just matches, but wooden ones that stayed lit better. I pocketed them along with the knife and took off again. But no luck. The cigarette bush was still green, the stalks not yet brown and hollow. It would be forever before it turned into anything that could be smoked. Still, I had some matches. I lit one and waved an index finger through it. No pain. I let it burn down to my finger and thumb then pinched the other end in my left hand so it could burn out completely. I lit another, made a wish, and blew it out. It soon occurred to me a campfire would be more fun than burning single matches, though.

I set to work gathering pine needles and twigs. Soon I had a nice dry pile shaped like a teepee. I dug around the edges, deep enough to get to moist earth that would contain the fire to this ring. Then I lit it. One match was all it took. It was a good fire. I put a few more twigs in. I stuck the knife blade in, pulled it out darkened, and thought about how much it would hurt to get branded. The fire burned fast and I needed more twigs than I had. Most of the fallen trees, stumps and branches were rotting and not dry enough to burn, but I had plenty of dry pine bark. All I really needed was one good-sized log or branch. I knew better than to pillage our firewood pile, but there was probably something nearby. I explored a little until I came to a whitened branch just lying in the sun like a gift from heaven. I ran back to my fire with it. Carefully building up the fire with the remaining twigs, I put the branch on top. It finally caught and I had a good little fire that I enjoyed for hours, or maybe just a couple of minutes. Then I was bored again. I wished I had a hot dog or something to stick in the fire. I was a little hungry. In fact, I was really hungry. I kicked the branch out of the fire, into the fresh dirt of the ring but there wasn't any water around for a long ways, not until the creek, and that was too far. I got a stick and flicked more dirt from the ring onto the branch. The flame died out. I put more dirt on the fire mound. I pulled a bunch of fresh green leaves and needles from trees so the moisture could smother the fire even more. It worked. It smoked bad, but the fire seemed pretty much out.

I ran back to the house. Breakfast had worn off and I was ready to eat again. I circled the house and came in through the front, screen door slapping behind me.

"Mothuuur," I called out.

"Quit yellin. I'm in the kitchen," she said in that *I don't want any mess* voice.

"I'm hungry."

"Your hands ain't painted on. Fix a samwitch."

She was soaking greens in the sink and peeling root vegetables, so supper was a long ways away. I got the Wonder Bread and mayonnaise out and sliced a tomato. I took my tomato sandwich to the table, eating quickly before the bread could get soggy. Mother brought over a glass of milk and sniffed.

"You smell smoke?"

I opened my eyes wide and sniffed hard. "Nope."

She looked around. She went to the window, pulling the curtain all the way to the side.

"Good Lord, smoke's coming up from the back woods. Run and get your daddy from the Armstrongs' and get Mr. Armstrong to come too. Tell them we got a fire in the back woods." She gave orders as she pulled out the mop pail. "Tell them bring shovels," she said, running out the back door.

It must have flared up after I left, or maybe a spark flew out and caught some dry leaves. It spread fast, moving towards Mr. Sample's property. Those woods went right up to his barn. Mrs. Armstrong had called neighbors up and down the road. Men and boys in pickups came with shovels and hoses. Mrs. Perry and a few other neighbor ladies clustered in the backyard talking, shaking their heads. Every now and then, smoke blew our way and made it even harder for me to breathe. No one was paying me any mind, but I stayed away from them anyway, close to the side yard where I could see everything, but out of speaking distance.

It felt like forever before they started coming back out of the woods, all the neighbor men, along with Mother and Daddy, grimy, looping hoses, lugging shovels. A man I didn't know said something to Daddy but I was too far away to hear, then they both stopped and turned to look back, just standing there for a while. I was petrified that it had flared back up again. But no, they turned back around and continued heading towards the house. So many blackened tree trunks. My mouth was dry.

At supper, the questioning came.

"Girl, you weren't out in the woods playing with matches, were you?" Mother turned to me after she and Daddy had speculated on how the fire started.

"No ma'am. I was in the front yard almost all day. Remember I came in the front door for a samwitch?" I had practiced this part, thinking how lucky it was I had come in the front instead of the back right before mother had spotted the smoke. For once, I was glad that Dare was having supper at one of his friend's house. He'd zero in on my cover in a minute, I knew.

"You sure you weren't playing with one of those magnifying glasses or something that could have caught pine needles on fire?" She looked at me hard.

"No ma'am. I lost that magnifying glass," I answered honestly.

"Well, looked like whoever lit it tried to put it out, too," Daddy said.

"I hope we don't have tramps passing through, camping in our woods," Mother said, turning to look at him. "Good thing I got a keen nose, or else who knows how far that fire might've spread. That barn is full of hay. That would have done Joe Sample in entirely. He's already just barely making do."

Then she turned and looked hard at me again. I couldn't swallow the collards in my mouth.

"Willa Mae, I don't want you messin' in those woods for a while, you hear me? Not unless your brother's with you."

"Yes ma'am."

"Don't just *yes ma'am* me. I mean it. I catch you in them woods any time soon and I'll tan your hide, hear me girl?"

"Yes ma'am," I said with more emphasis.

She turned to my father. "You and Harlan ought to take a look out there 'fore Willie goes running wild this summer. See if there are other campfires been put out back there."

They exchanged a long, silent look.

Long before the reeds had time to hollow, I was back in the woods making fires. More than anything, more than even a chance to go hunting with Dare, I wanted to meet a tramp. I moved my camp spot closer to the creek where I could easily fill coffee cans of water to douse any embers, and I wrote in black ash on the wood fence behind Sample's barn, **TRAMPS WELCOME**. I made up hobo names for myself to cover my trail after I took off with my new companion so I wouldn't get caught. Moonshine Mack. Will Freeloader. Micky Ember. Late at night, when I heard the train in the distance, I could almost hear him hopping off as it slowed at the crossroads, and I willed him to come to the woods where I would make the best campfire ever. We would smoke and carve our initials into trees before we lit out.

Beloved Angel

The Sample family graveyard was a favorite haunt of mine. From the woods behind their barn, if I followed the field drainage ditch that Dare and me called a creek up to the blacktop, it was just across the road. Because of the trees, I could walk right over to the graveyard without being seen from any house nearby, even when I was crossing the road. There were three magnolias inside the wrought iron fence, one as tall as a skyscraper, with limbs low enough that it was easy to climb. Together, the three trees kept the little patch of graves shaded and cool. Some graves were sunken in a little, some markers were just simple wooden crosses so deteriorated that I didn't dare sneeze near them. I was careful to walk around the graves, not over them, but it was so unkempt that it was hard to tell sometimes whether a patch was a grave or not.

There was one grave that I went to more than the others, even more than the mother and baby ones that always drew me. It was the Beloved Angel tombstone of Beverly Ann Sample, who had died in the 1800s. On top, it said **BELOVED ANGEL ON THE WINGS OF TIME** written in fancy cursive. Below that was **BEVERLY ANN SAMPLE 1880-1890** and under that was **OUR BELOVED ANGEL, CARRIED ON THE SWIFT WINGS OF TIME, HOME TO GOD'S ARMS**. It was practically a book compared to most headstones.

It struck me on one particular day that Beverly and I were the same age—ten years old. It started me wondering what would it be like to be ten in 1890. And then to die. I pictured her with pigtails, wearing an old timey dress like the drawings in *Little Women* in the bookcase at home. Under the filtered light of that big magnolia, I sat there and pondered her life. Were there tractors, or would she have been in the field with her whole family, plowing and reaping by hand? I wished I knew the details of her story. What could kill a ten-year-old? As full of words as the tombstone was, there was no clue to how she died. Some of the markers told a plain story. The baby graves, usually just a small stone lying flat in the ground giving the dates, mostly in months, were clear. They died getting born or soon after. One was a mother and baby side by side. The baby, not even with a name or life span dates, just *and daughter*, told a clear tale. The mother died having that baby and nobody even bothered to give her a name, and no graveyard sweetness either, no *beloved* or anything. Seemed liked the dad was mad at the baby when he buried them.

Babies were one thing, but a ten-year-old girl was entirely different. Somebody that old could pretty much take care of herself. So, what had happened? Had she got one of them diseases that kids now get vaccinated for? Had she got mangled up in some farm machinery? Awful things like that happened to farm kids a lot. I didn't know a single farmer that didn't have something missing, if only a half of a finger. There was that farmer at church who had a leg missing below the knee, and I'd heard he had two fake legs, one for everyday use, and the other a "dress up" leg that he wore to church. I'd stared at the real shoe on his wooden foot in church more than once.

"Beverly Ann Sample," I gave myself goosebumps addressing the dead girl. "What happened to you?"

It felt funny to be talking out loud in the graveyard. I felt sorry for Beverly Ann, who had been dead for about 100 years. Then the ground tilted a little. Not quite 100 years. I never did like arithmetic. I tried to do it in my head but couldn't. I scratched some figures above my ashy kneecap. She died in 1890 and it was 1965 now. Minus the 1890 from 1965. That wasn't 100, it was 75 years ago. I did it twice to make sure I had carried the numbers right. She would have been 85 if she had lived. I knew for a fact that some of the ladies in my church were that old. I felt a funny spinning feeling. I had come here and looked at this grave so many times and thought about the dead girl from another century. She might have made it from that century to this one if only she hadn't died at ten. It was unsettling how the distance between us seemed to shrink. The girl in pigtails that I sort of knew could be a white-haired old woman in a patterned dress with pictures of grandbabies in her pocketbook. I had read the tombstones with the 1800 dates as if they were part of the long ago, the unknowable world. But suddenly that faraway time just got strangely connected to the now because there were people still walking around who had been in both.

Then another crazy thought struck me. If I don't die, if I live to be 85 years old, I might be part of a different world. I used my leg again to add 1965 + 75 but it wasn't coming out right. 2040 wasn't a real year. I did it over and over, and it kept coming out 2040. It *would* be a year. The thought of a year starting with 20 instead of 19 was unbelievable, something made up, like *The Jetsons* or *Lost in Space.* Maybe fun to imagine, but definitely not real. But then every single day of my life up until today, Beverly Ann Sample was someone who could never have existed in my world because she was from another century. It was hard to get a handle on it. Beverly could be some old lady in church. I might live into a time past the 1900s, into another century, as foreign and strange as a past century has always been.

My temple was throbbing a little with an idea that couldn't quite take shape. It was about time. It was the way that Beverly had connected the far away to the now and the way the now was going to move forward, carrying me with it whether I wanted to go or not, closer to some hazy place that I couldn't even picture. Just like I didn't know whether Beverly took baths in a real bathtub or in some wash tub with hot water poured from off the kitchen stove, I couldn't see what was ahead of me, and for the first time ever, I fretted about that. I had only thought about time in practical ways before: time for dinner, close to Christmas, time for school to let out. But there was this whole other feature that couldn't be seen, and yet, it was the real truth of time. Time connected things like links in a chain, and it went backwards and forwards as far as the mind could see. It stretched at some point into eternity, where people were in heaven or hell.

That made me think of Beverly again. She was in eternity, out of this graveyard that had numbers marking centuries. She was either in heaven or hell. I could feel the dread welling in me. If she had lived long enough she would undoubtedly be saved. Old people are always saved. But she was ten. I knew I wasn't a good Christian, and I wasn't really sure of my spot in heaven, but I always figured on having some time before that was critical. Now, I hoped fiercely that Beverly had been saved before she died. I prayed before I thought about it, "God, please let Beverly have been saved." But could it even work like that? Could God change something if it had already happened? She'd been dead a long time.

Then I was conscious of God looking at me and that made me feel cautious. Like maybe I should get out of the graveyard and go home. It didn't seem wrong to keep figuring out how time worked, though, and that occupied my thoughts back across the road and through the woods on the way home. I took a long, looping path back towards the house. In my mind, I could see Mother in the kitchen and me coming in to make a sandwich. I could see that time had already changed me even though I looked like the same Willie who left the house only a few hours ago. Mother wouldn't notice, her shoulders curved over the sink in one of the endless kitchen chores. I could see this as if it were happening. And just barely, I could see a completely different me, a stranger, in a far-off time. Inside we're made up of the time that has passed, but still every second moves us into to the mystery ahead, changing us with each step. Time was like the Holy Spirit. You couldn't see it, but it moved in and around us, invisible as air, always operating on the visible world.

Long Distance

Mother had two sisters, Aunt Etta and Aunt Ouncey, whose real name was Louellen. She was born early and small. From day one they called her Ouncey because she hardly weighed a pound, or so the story goes. Everyone treated her like she still might not live. Aunt Ouncey was crazy about me and Dare. She was always trying to get Mother to send us to Georgia for a visit.

We were forbidden from answering the phone if she called, though. That was on account of the time that Dare picked up and stayed on the line with her for almost an hour when she was having a bad spell. It wasn't just the phone bill Mother had worried about. Mother was the only one that could soothe Aunt Ouncey out of her bad spells, probably because Mother was the oldest and had helped raise her two younger sisters. She felt responsible for them, but especially for Aunt Ouncey, who Mother said was high strung. Even so, it was never clear exactly how we were supposed to know if it was her on the line before we picked up.

That's why when I heard the phone ringing as I walked in the back door, I ran to answer it. What else could I do? I wasn't even really thirsty. I just wanted to quit working in the garden for a while, so I told Mother I needed a drink of water. She was still out there pulling weeds. Even as I said *hello*, words rushed at me, mid-sentence and indecipherable, but I picked up Aunt Ouncey's Georgia twang.

" . . . Before that I was nearly drowned to death," she raced on. "That was when I met Wild Bill Hickok, and you know I almost married him. . . ." I could hardly believe my ears. I thought about Uncle Clayton, his big farmer hands, broad-knuckled and seamed. I wondered if he knew about Wild Bill before he married her. But she hadn't stopped talking.

Her words hurtled on, and there was something about the high pitch of her voice and the speed of the words, like she was trying to get everything out that she needed to say before rushing out the door that let me know that she was in one of her bad spells. I knew I wasn't supposed to be talking to her but wasn't sure what to do about it. Dare had told me that when he was on the phone with her for almost an hour that she had said cuss words. I never believed it. My mother's family did not cuss.

"Aunt Ouncey? It's Willie. You want me to go get Mother? She's in the garden." I tried to make her hear me but she just kept going, didn't even give me a chance to interrupt.

" . . . In those days, I rode horses like an Indian. No saddle. I flew, that's what I did. And they gave me a Cherokee name that no one else could use, but a bear stole it from me during a harvest moon. . . ." I was enthralled. I tried to puzzle out how a bear steals a name, but her words just kept galloping on, faster and higher. She had taken a long ride back to Wild Bill when I heard Mother coming up the back steps. I froze.

When Mother came into the kitchen, I said, "Hello?" like I had just picked up the phone. Then, "Hello? Is this Aunt Ouncey?"

Mother was beside me in an instant, looking hard at me and reaching for the phone. I handed it to her and she turned her back and stood up straighter as she heard the voice at the other end.

"Ouncey, honey? It's Mary. Slow down, sis. Slow down, OK? Shh, shh, quiet now." She started crooning into the phone like she was calming a fretting baby. "Is Clayton there, honey? I need you to look around and tell me where Clayton is, OK? Is he home?"

I sidled toward the cabinet and got one of the jelly jars we used for glasses as quietly as I could but just held it, knowing if I turned the spigot on Mother would hear and turn around.

"Shh, now. No horses, OK? Listen, Ouncey, you look out

your window and see whether Clayton's in the fields or the yard, hear me?" She spoke so softly it gave me a pang.

"He's out back? Good girl, Ouncey. Shh. Listen. This is very important. Understand? It's very important that you walk straight to Clayton and tell him Mary is on the phone to talk to him. Don't go anywhere else, OK? Go straight to Clayton and tell him. Don't hang up. Leave the phone on the counter and bring Clayton to the phone." Mother said it slow and kept repeating things, not like she usually talked. She sighed, and turning toward the kitchen sink, noticed me.

"Go on outside, Willie," she said in a flat, tired voice.

"I'm thirsty," I said, turning on the spigot and letting the water run until it cooled a little.

"Drink that and get outside." She sounded more irritated this time.

I took as long as I could without getting into trouble, but apparently neither Aunt Ouncey or Uncle Clayton had made it back to the phone. Finally, I had to just skulk out the back door. The midday heat blazed. I made my way towards the backyard to sit under the big tree that Daddy had put the tire swing on, thinking I could put off weeding the garden until Mother came back. I ran my fingers through the sparse grass checking for four leaf clovers.

I thought about Aunt Ouncey's crazy talk and the way Mother spoke to her, like a child, and a dim-witted one at that, but soft, with a tenderness that made me feel close to tears. I wished I could go stay at the farm with Aunt Ouncey, where Uncle Clayton would let us ride in his lap on the tractor. Mother was different when we went there. She and Aunt Ouncey laughed and told old stories until late at night, long after we'd been made to go to bed. She called Ouncey "Lou Lou," and "honey," and "stinkpot," in a soft way that made me want her to turn to me with the same voice. I hoped Aunt Ouncey had done what she was supposed to do and had gotten Uncle Clayton and brought him to the phone. It was funny hearing her talk about getting a Cherokee name and almost marrying Wild Bill Hickok, but I knew I shouldn't laugh. I knew something was wrong. I hoped she wasn't going crazy, and as soon as that thought took shape, I felt panicky. It was enough to propel me toward prayer, that rare and uncomfortable effort that I generally avoided except at bedtime or out of fear of the Rapture.

But I did it for her. I whispered fiercely towards my kneecaps "Dear Lord, forgive me for my sins and please help Aunt Ouncey not be crazy." Then, because I felt like God was probably looking now, I made my way back to the rows of squash, to the place where I had left off weeding. I hated the furry, itchy leaves that I had to reach under to pull out the weeds and grass. I sat back on my haunches to complete the row I'd been set to do before Aunt Ouncey's high-speed voice had galloped all this way. I thought she probably hadn't almost married Wild Bill Hickok, but maybe she had dreamed about it. And I hoped, I really hoped, that she still had a Cherokee name that lived somewhere and that she would find it again.

Shillin Town

The single best thing that I ever figured out on my own was that you could do a lot of stuff if you just don't ask permission first. When no one has expressly said no, as long as you don't get caught, there's no problem. Taking off down the blacktop, I called back to the bobwhites as I pedaled away. Were they answering me, or just continuing their own private conversation? If they were answering, what were they saying? *Good morning? Worms over here? Watch out there, girl on the bike?* The endless field on the left was tall with corn that day. The houses on the right were knit together by the kudzu covering the woody patches between them. A nest of rusted out trucks decayed beside a barn with a slumped roof, an old tractor visible inside. Shirts flapped on a clothesline. I felt it all. I was everything around me—the clacking bike chain, the waving clothes, the air parting around me and moving through me, the sunlight illuminating a world that I was seamlessly etched into. I wanted to ride without stopping.

When I got out to where the Weaver family lived in a house flanked by several trailers that had been added to the lot for the older kids who had married, I paused. I had never gone past that spot before. The road forked ahead. The left continued along the Dismal Swamp route, farther out into the country, vast expanses of fields with the occasional farmhouse, a Sunday drive route. To the right was a winding road that eventually connected to the highway that led to the ocean. I stood anchored with one foot on the ground, the other on the pedal, wishing I could ride my bike far enough to be at the beach. That was another world—the salty air and screaming gulls, the way the waves lifted you up and crashed over you, the shoreline filled with burrowing sand fiddlers and sand that changed colors as the water came up and washed out. But that was impossible on a bike. It seemed to take forever even in a car. I wheeled around and headed back down the road.

The euphoria of being part of everything receded. I was just going back the same way I came. I started practicing my whistling with a song we learned in school that year, "The Streets of Laredo." Then I belted it out, happy at how loud my voice was in the quiet. *As I headed out to the streets of Laredo, as I headed out to Laredo one daaaay. . . . I spied a young cowboy wrapped in white linen, wrapped in white linen and cold as the claaaay. . . .*

There were places where I almost caught an echo. I hoped people in their houses could hear me and would wonder who that girl was singing down the road. I weaved my bike between the yellow dashes on the road since no cars were coming. I looked up and noticed the turnoff to Shillin Town Road, where the colored people in the area lived. I knew they had their own store and church, but I wasn't even sure how I knew that. It wasn't like folks talked about it. I had passed the turnoff a million times in the car and even sometimes on my bike, but white people didn't go down there, so I'd never seen the town. Not even thinking about why I shouldn't, I crossed the road to go to Shillin Town. My heart thumped hard when I turned off the pavement onto the dirt lane. At first, there was nothing more than country with trees on either side, but I could hear kids' voices in the distance, laughing and playing. The first place I passed was a ramshackle old house. I thought it might be abandoned. Then I thought I saw a hint of movement on the partially screened porch, but it could have been a flap of torn screen lifted by wind. When I rounded the first curve, I could see kids ahead playing in the middle of the lane. Some were kicking a ball around in the dirt. One of them, a girl about my age, looked up and saw me. She froze. Then they all looked towards me. I raised my hand, waving, but they were already darting across ditches and disappearing into yards and houses. I had started to call out *Hey* as I waved but the word died in my throat, never making it out of my mouth. The girl who had first seen me had flat out disappeared. Had she even seen me wave? A little kid, still in diapers, sat in a yard near where the kickball game had been going on. I watched as an older girl came out, hoisted him onto her hip, and was back in the house in a blink. I knew I had caused this, but I wasn't sure why everyone had cleared out. All the shouting and laughter I'd heard when I first turned down the lane was silenced. It was unnatural quiet. I could hear my breath. I could hear my tires on the dirt, but I couldn't hear the people who had just been there minutes ago. I thought maybe if I hummed they would see I was peaceful, but I couldn't get a noise out of my dry throat.

I hadn't known this was a dead-end road. I saw that now, as I looked ahead and could see that there was a church in the distance that this road led smack dab into. There wasn't a steeple, but there was a big cross on the peak of the A-frame, so there was no question about where I'd end up if I rode to the end. *I'll U-turn at the church and try to pick up speed on the way out.* The air seemed to buzz. It was like I was riding in a ghost town, but somehow I was the ghost. I could feel eyes on me. Every window seemed to be watching. I worked hard to make enough spit to swallow. I knew I'd messed up.

Out of nowhere—an explosion by my leg—a dog thundered, barking, snarling, berserk. I saw him from the corner of my eye and veered so sharp that I skidded and fell hard. I was dead. But I opened my eyes a squint and saw that he was on a chain that was choking him as he lunged and barked with his teeth bared and ears pinned back. He was frantic. So was I. In one quick move, I was up and pedaling furiously, racing the sound of that dog trying to break free and eat me alive. I didn't stop flying full speed even when I hit the paved road. Only later did two thoughts take shape in my head: *good thing no car was coming* and *did I hear laughing?*

By the time the Sample farmhouse was in sight, I was pedaling normal and my breath had evened out. I turned towards the tractor path that would take me to the Sample graveyard in the field. I needed some time to settle. I laid my bike down outside the wrought iron fence, let myself inside and sat under the big magnolia. I could still hear my heart pounding in my head. Why had I done that? I knew white people didn't go down Shillin Town Road, even if I didn't really know why. Now what if someone finds out and tells Mother? Right beside that panicked thought was a shadow thrill, *I know what it looks like in Shillin Town. I've been there and seen it.* The lane and houses weren't that much different than down most country roads. There were gardens in the backyards just like everywhere else. There were old cars on side lots and a church. But I hadn't seen a store. There's supposed to be a store there, too. I felt it start to happen inside, the first needling of wanting to go back. Out loud I said *no.* No way I'm going back and giving that dog a second chance. There was a store even if I didn't see it. And I'm safe from getting in trouble because who would there be to tell Mother? No one. No white people houses are close enough to have seen me coming out of Shillin Town Road and back on the pavement. The other houses along the way I pass all the time. Why would anyone give it a second thought? They wouldn't. I was safe.

Then I thought of the girl, the first one to see me, before everyone evaporated. Why had she looked at me that way? Didn't she see me wave? And why didn't she wave back? It was like she was scared of me, but I wasn't any bigger than her. Her running off made me feel ashamed. I wouldn't have been mean. I would have played kickball, too, if they'd invited me. Was it a rule for them not to play with anyone they didn't know, or just white people? Would I have gotten them in trouble? I knew my invasion had busted up their game. I wasn't welcome.

That night, she floated back up in my head as I was lying in bed waiting for sleep. She took on a name, Lela, because I liked the sound of it. We sat and talked under a tree up near the turnoff, just a little ways off the blacktop, between the two places. It was unclear whether Lela had a bike, so we decided to spy in Shillin Town. We slipped from backyard to backyard. She showed me the store and listed the candy they sold—root beer barrels, licorice, candy necklaces, Bazooka bubble gum, Fireballs, Pixy Stix. As soon as we got some money, we'd come back and get some bubble gum. We'd see who could blow the biggest bubble with it. She steered me clear of Killer, the rabid dog. We clapped out Mrs. Mary Mack, and Oh Little Playmate, and Long-Legged Sailor. She smiled a lot when she talked and her front two teeth were bigger than her other ones, with a gap in between. We promised we'd always be friends. We shook on it.

Miss Alma's Sugar

Dare was cutting grass when I got up, but before I got dressed and had breakfast he was already off on his bike to meet the stupid boys in Feral. I hated them, that bunch of sweaty, stinking finks. I didn't really know them since they went to school in town, but I still hated them. I went to the backyard and climbed on top of the tire swing, not inside its O, holding the rope, pushing off from the tree. The air smelled like fresh-cut grass. In the distance, a mourning dove made its lonesome call. A blue jay cawed an insult over my head. I made a pistol with my thumb and forefinger and shot it. I pushed myself away from the tree and back, a human pendulum, not really thinking about anything, not allowing myself to miss Dare. The sound of wheels on gravel perked me up. Someone had come to visit. I hopped off the swing and ran to the front yard. Miss Alma's big boat of a car was pulling up in the center of the U. I ran to open her car door for her. She heaved herself out in a series of moves and grunts. She was a big woman with a lot of belly. I was so glad to have something to do that I smiled right up at her.

"Hey, Miss Alma. How you?" It sounded fake even to my own ears, but she smiled broadly at me.

"Well, I'm just fine, Wilhelmina Mae. I got a bag of snap beans for your mama in the back seat there. You want to carry it in for me, sugar?"

"Sure." Why did the church ladies always have to say that long stupid name instead of Willie?

"Been so hot lately, I ain't wanted to work in the garden. Got out there early this morning and things look like they just growing wild. I brought in what I could and did a little weeding, but that's enough for one day. I ought to be putting up some pickles soon."

On the other hand, I did like it when the church ladies talked to me the same way they did to my mother, like I knew all about house stuff or growing pole beans.

"Yes ma'am," I said. "I love pickles."

Miss Alma laughed and patted my shoulder. The church ladies are in a world apart. You can never tell what will make them laugh, or make their eyes water, or make them shake their heads like they simply don't understand what English just came out your mouth.

We got up to the steps and Mother was already at the door, holding it open.

"Well, hello, Alma. Good to see you," she said.

"I been doing some garden work and brought you some snap beans. I hope I'm not catching you at a bad time."

"Oh no, not at all. I was just about to sit down and have some coffee. I hope you can stay for a while."

"Just for a little bit. Long enough for some coffee, I reckon."

I knew what that meant. They'd be at the table for hours probably, talking about what was in the papers and gossiping about every neighbor and church lady they knew. If I played my cards right, I could probably lurk long enough to catch something I wasn't supposed to hear. I put the paper bag full of beans on the kitchen counter. I knew better than to even try sitting at the table.

"Willie, bring over some Pet milk out of the fridge for Miss Alma," Mother said, pouring coffee.

I took my time finding it.

"You know, Mary, your Wilhelmina Mae has grown like a weed! She'll be a young lady before you know it. She's got nice manners, too, not like some young'uns I could name."

Mother smiled and lifted her cup. "Well, Lord knows we try. She's willful but she can be a good girl when she sets her mind to it."

I could feel my face flush, but I knew if I hovered too long Mother would give me the *go on outside and play now* and I didn't feel like sitting in the dirt under the Nandina bush today on the chance that they'd have good gossip. Instead, I slipped around toward the living room and pulled out the *Look* magazine Miss Alma had brung over on her last visit. I lay on my belly, on the other side of the wall that separated the kitchen and living room. If for some reason Mother came in, I'd just be looking at a magazine.

"Hard to imagine that by the time that girl gets into high school it will be integrated," Alma sighed.

"Well at least it will be a nice new school. They've been building on it for how long now? Last time we rode by it looked huge. The gym building alone is 'bout as big as Central."

"Well, Lester says they've been building it so long to be in some sort of standing with the state or maybe it's the federal gov'ment, I'm not sure. But anyhow, they need to show we're in compliance with that law. Lester says if we're smart, it'll take at least another ten years before it's built. Give us some time to try and make things right. But then I read in the paper it's due to open in two years. Any way you look at it, it's bound to happen. Not like a pool or park that you can just shut down." She made a *tsk*ing sound with her tongue on her teeth.

"Let me get you some more coffee, Alma. You know, Willie had that boy in her class this year. They got several coloreds in the school now already, one's in her class. Seems like it's going alright. To tell the truth, that's how I thought they'd go about it, pick the right ones and slowly keep adding them in and everything'll work out OK. They're not all troublemakers. Good ones know how to act and there hasn't been a lick of trouble with the ones they let in."

"Maybe not, but look here, how many them you think will be going to high school same time as Wilhelmina? There won't be another high school for them to go to, then. That's the thing. Every kid that's going to high school in Feral or out here will be going to that new school. Every single one. It's plain scary when you really think about it. Look down the road from here, down Shillin Town. How many of them right there, right down the road? Every one of them living there will be going to that school. That's not even counting all the other areas. And you know they have so many babies, every colored woman I know got at least five. It's a shame, it really is. All on account of Yankees thinking they know how to run things better'n us when they don't know squat. Ain't caused nothing but trouble. People don't even know how to act any more these days."

"Well now, that *is* the Lord's truth. Seem like folks can't even be decent these days. I was at the Winn Dixie the other day at the register, thought I was finished with my shopping until I realized I forgot to pick up any bacon, and when I asked the bag boy if he could run back and grab it for me, he rolled his eyes at me! I couldn't believe it myself. No *yes ma'am* or anything civil, just rolled his eyes then dragged his feet down the aisles. That girl at the register, she didn't even say a word about it neither. Those spoiled little city kids they got working summers there now just don't know how to act. I reckon all we can do is make sure our own children know how to behave when they're out in the world."

Miss Alma gave a deep sigh. "Well, my boys are almost graduated, but I tell you what, I'd take money out from the house and send them to private school, even a Catholic one, before I'd send them to a school that was almost all nig— coloreds. And they're boys. If the Lord had blessed me with a little girl, I sure wouldn't send her off to spend the day around a bunch of colored bucks straight out of the fields. No siree."

I heard Miss Alma correct herself before using a bad word, but not before it was clear what she would have said. Mother and Birdy didn't agree on much but they were clear as a June day on one thing: there's never good cause to talk ugly. I almost felt sorry for Miss Alma, slipping up like that in front of Mother.

"Well, sufficient to the day is the evil thereof. Who knows what's going to happen next year, much less in five. I got a while before that's one of the worries I need to settle." I heard Mother set her coffee cup in the saucer the sharp way she did when she had given her final word on some subject. Seemed like Miss Alma didn't get it, though, because she kept on going.

"Well, at least Dare's at school with Wilhelmina Mae for now and he can keep an eye on her, protect her if need be. But he won't be around for her whole time in high school."

Mother let out something like a snort. "Protect her? Half the time it's him she needs protecting from. I swan, he had her out by the ditch the other day, he'd talked her into standing there while he was on the other side throwing knives at her feet to see how close he could get without cutting a toe off. I tanned his hide right smart about that. Never thought Willie'd be that dumb, though. That girl can usually fight her own battles."

That stung me. Mother didn't even know the rules for chicken and she just didn't even know that she didn't know, and she was calling *me* dumb. She was the one that didn't get it. Though it *was* true that Dare never let me throw knives at his feet, so it wasn't exactly equal, not like when we rode bikes toward each other full speed to see who would swerve first. These days, though, I'd play by his rules when he was home long enough to do things with me instead of the Feral boys. I had pushed the magazine out in front of me and Mother must have heard it.

"Is that you, Willie?" she called.

"I was just looking at a magazine." I got to my feet, magazine in hand.

"Come on in here and give me some sugar before I head back home," Miss Alma said.

"Do you have to go already, Alma? Won't you stay for a while? At least let me give you some of the early strawberries we got from the garden." I knew if Mother really wanted her to stay she would have offered her strawberry shortcake at the table and not some cut up strawberries in a jar to take with her. I wondered if Miss Alma knew, too.

"No, I better get on back before Lester thinks I done run off. But I can't say no to strawberries. Thank you kindly." She laughed softly and put an arm out to me, inviting me in for a hug. I didn't really like getting that close to old ladies, especially knowing she'd end up kissing my cheek, but I felt sorry for her somehow. It seemed like maybe she had been standing up for me when my own mother had just called me dumb. Plus, I was a little embarrassed for her since she almost said a bad word in front of Mother, and I knew how Mother could cut a person down with her eyes. I wondered what it would be like to be Miss Alma's daughter instead of Mother's. I walked into her open arm and allowed her to fold me into her. Instead of her kissing my cheek, though, I stood on tiptoe and pressed my lips very softly against Miss Alma's dry, powdery cheek.

"Well aren't you just the sweetest little girl." Her eyes got a little watery as she looked down at me. I smiled up at her and opened my eyes wide. I could see Mother, eyebrows raised, looking over from putting a jar of sliced strawberries in a lunch bag. She had a crooked smile, like she was making fun of something, but she didn't say a word.

"I'm heading up the food and drinks for Vacation Bible School this summer, Mary. I know I can always count on your help. I'll be calling you 'bout that in a week or so. Last year it seemed like some of those children hadn't eaten for a month when it was time for cold drinks and food," Miss Alma said on the way to the door.

"You just let me know what you need, Alma. I'd be willing to come in one day, too, and help serve, if need be."

"Well, thank you for the coffee. Give my best to Walter. And as for you," she leaned down and took my chin in her hand, "You're a good little girl. You could come live with me any day and be right welcome." She smacked a kiss on my cheek.

"You better watch out, or I just might send her on over there," Mother said, dry as toast.

I watched the car pull out the getaway side of the U and felt a little sorry for myself. Family was supposed to stick together, but it seemed like Mother had been making fun of me in front of Miss Alma. I didn't like it a bit. Then saying "I might send her over there," like that would be something terrible. I wandered back towards the swing, mad at Mother and vowing not to go in the house until she called out the back door at suppertime. I hadn't even heard much good stuff. Miss Alma was always fired up about the integration. I wasn't clear on what it was, other than the colored kids from Shillin Town would go to the same school as all the white kids. I was secretly happy about that. We all rode the same school bus, only they got dropped off at Booker T. Washington after the white kids got left off at Central. I always wished it was the other way around so I could see their school. A lot of the grown-ups were riled up about the integration, but there were things they just didn't get. Like Mother not understanding how chicken works, it wasn't just Dare throwing knives at my toes like she said. I climbed up on the swing and pictured the school I'd seen under construction between town and here. It was already bigger than Central and it wasn't even done yet. I didn't want to go to school with the city kids, though. They were snobby; you could bank on that. The grown-ups were always talking about the fights that were going to bust out during the integration. We had fights already, though. The kids would make a circle around the fighters and yell for the one they were pulling for, until a teacher, a P.E. teacher usually, came and busted it up.

Then I got it. I pictured a colored boy and a white boy fighting. It gave me a squirrely feeling in my gut. It wouldn't be fair. I just knew it. It wouldn't be fair even if the colored boy won, *especially* if the colored boy won. Something bad *would* happen. I pushed myself away from the tree hard as I could, and back, and away. I pulled back on the rope, lifting my face to the sky, jerking my course around.

In September, I would start fifth grade. I would go back to Central. We would hate and make fun of the city kids at Roosevelt, but we never talked about the kids at Booker T. We didn't scrimmage against them. The football team never played them. Theirs was a different world, existing in the seams, not clearly visible. For the first time since hearing about the integration I felt a little scared. Maybe the grown-ups were right this time, maybe bad things were going to happen. I pushed hard off the tree again and even though I wasn't praying, I said between my teeth, *just keep it fair, the fights and everything else, keep it fair.*

Locket

I found a dime between the couch cushions before bedtime. I put it in a double hiding place—inside my locket, in my jewelry box. The box had a tiny pink ballerina on a spring that popped up and spun around to "Swan Lake" when the lid opened. I closed and rewound it.

Lazing in bed the next morning, I pulled the thin cotton sheet up to my chin while weighing my options. I could ride to the store and get wax lips, Fireballs, maybe some Pixy Stix. I could go the other way to Culpepper's Print Shop just past the Armstrongs' and get a Coca-Cola from their machine. Coke was rare at home and when we did get them, Mother would pour one bottle into two glasses, careful to make it even, so Dare and I could share. A whole Coke to myself won out.

It was still early enough that there was dew on the ground. The cool prickly grass felt good on my bare feet. I had what Mother called my "summer feet" by then, so leathery I could go anywhere without shoes, even the gravel in the driveway didn't faze me. I ran across the front yard, jumped the ditch, and veered left. The pavement wasn't even hot yet. The locket lay flat on my chest, partially visible in the V of my buttoned-up sleeveless summer shirt.

Culpepper's Print Shop was a squat little brick building. Three broad steps led up to the wooden porch. It was never very busy. The boards creaked under my feet as I walked over to the bright red machine, pulling my locket up and prying it open for the coin. The only choice was Coke, a whole row of them. The machine kept them ice cold. I put the dime in the slot, pushed the button, and down it clunked, that shapely, green-hued bottle. I used the bottle opener on the machine that dropped the cap into some tinny recess.

No one seemed to be around, so I sat on the top step looking across the fields and took my first heady swig. The bubbles tickled my nose. There was nothing better than this. Unless it was this and a moon pie. The corn in the field was tall and green. I felt grown, sitting there with my Coke in hand, surveying the scenery. The morning was heating up but I took my time.

When I eventually got up to put the empty bottle in the crate, a man came out of the dim interior, screen door slapping behind him. He was baggy—baggy eyes, baggy trousers, baggy shirt. He was looking my way with bleary, unfocused eyes. I hadn't expected to see anyone. I froze. He scratched at the front of his pants near his zipper. My cheeks burned and I dropped my eyes. He shuffled closer. My mouth went a little dry, like when you have to vomit. He reached a shaky hand toward me, and before I knew it he had lifted the locket. He leaned in and put his other hand flat on my chest, like he was balancing himself or something.

"Purdy necklace, girlie." His breath was a gale of dead fish smell.

Then he looked at me a little closer from underneath his puffy lids. I was still frozen, but this time I didn't drop my eyes.

"What's yer name, then?" Another wave of stink. The way he talked sounded like he had walked out of some dark past.

"Cat got yer tongue?" He was still holding my locket and his hand on my chest had grown heavier, a stone weight.

"No sir," my voice came out shaky. Grown-up men didn't usually pay much attention to kids, and I'd never known one to act like this. He looked like he'd slept in his clothes. This close up I could see the map of blood vessels all across his bulgy nose, see his yellowed bloodshot eyes.

"Roy!" A man's voice yelled from inside. "Get on back in here. I've called Mildred to come pick you up."

He was still looking at me. Then he gave me this crazy grin, like we'd just laughed at a joke. He slowly slid his one hand down off me, and the other let the locket fall back into place. He turned slightly, as if to go back in, and it was like some release lever got pulled because suddenly I wasn't frozen anymore. I flew off the steps and was halfway down the dirt driveway when the screen door slapped again. I didn't look back.

Back in my room, I opened the jewelry box. The little ballerina sprang up and twirled in circles. Round and round she went. I dropped the locket into its felt section and waited. I let the music wind down. The ballerina slowed, then jerked to an ungraceful halt. I closed and latched the lid without rewinding it.

Buttercup Chain

Dare's Daisy BB gun was all mine now. Maybe I shot at birds sometimes, but I never killed one. Probably. At least, I never saw one fall. Our picture window killed more birds than me. They'd fly into it with a sharp thud, and fall stunned into the gladiolas. Lucky ones would wake up a little later and flap uncertainly off. Unlucky ones usually got picked up by neighborhood cats or other night wanderers.

I loved Daisy, loved that the gun had a girl name. Walking in the woods toward the Sample property, I popped off a few shots, not aiming, just pointing the barrel between trees. I didn't have any Coke bottles today. I liked the cold ping it made when the BBs hit that target. I dreamed of having a real gun. I kept on the path until I got to the ditch that bordered Mr. Sample's farm, then decided to do some spying on his place. When I got close enough, I saw there was an old station wagon in the long dirt driveway. Old Man Sample's daughter was visiting. I stalked the edges of the property, moving from one tree to another, Daisy pulled up vertically at my side. When I got close enough that I could've thrown a rock and hit the car, the sharp slap of the screen door sent a jolt of panic through me. I could hear my heart beating inside my head. But it was only Sample's grandkids that had burst out the door, with their mother's voice trailing after them, "Y'all stay in the side yard and don't you dare go in that barn or I'll skin you alive!" There were three of them. The tallest was a girl but she was still just a kid, not nearly as old as me. The two littlest, dressed like boys, were chasing and pushing each other, whooping and hollering. The girl with straw-colored hair wandered over past the small garden to where a clump of buttercups was growing. She'll make a chain, I thought, rolling my eyes. Then she sat down in the grass and began to do just that. I slipped back tree to tree, heart racing, a plan forming in my head as I circled around to where she sat. When I got as close as I could without coming out into the open, I whistled. The girl took no notice. Was she deaf or stupid or something?

"Hey you! Hey you stupid girl," I stage whispered to get the girl's attention.

When she turned her head around, I stuck the barrel of the BB gun out from behind the tree, pointed at her. "Come on over here, girl."

The girl looked confused, but got up slowly, the beginnings of a buttercup chain in hand, and came within three steps of the tree.

"Halt! Right there. Don't come no further," I commanded. "Sit back down and face the house."

She obeyed and I stared at her slack-jawed profile, considering what to do next.

"Who're you?" she asked in a timid country voice.

"I'm your worst nightmare, that's who." That was something I'd heard Dare say, and I felt the thrill of the words on my tongue.

"But what's your name?" The girl didn't seem to get it. She didn't seem to know enough to even be scared. She just sat there, looking straight ahead toward the farmhouse like she was in a trance. Maybe she was simple.

"You see this here gun?"

"Can I look that way now?"

"Yes. Look over here then go back to looking at the house."

She turned and stared at the barrel of the BB gun then looked up at me. Her eyes were pale blue and her skin was sandy and freckled. Her dress was so faded and thin it ought to have been in the rag basket by now. The girl didn't seem at all nervous or scared like she should've been. She looked like someone walking in her sleep, sort of blank.

"You're my prisoner," I hissed.

When the girl didn't say anything, just kept looking vacantly at me, I kicked the tree. Then to show I meant business, I pumped the gun a few times and shot into the clump of buttercups. The girl jumped and made a squeaky noise. That was more like it.

"You're going to do what I say, or I'm going to shoot you. You understand me, girl?"

"Yes ma'am."

I might have thought she was being a smart aleck except her voice came out a little shaky and nervous. The girl really must be simple, calling me *ma'am* as if I were a grown-up. I decided to let it go.

"Now you come over here and give me that buttercup chain. Wait! First finish making it into a circle. Then come on over here and drop it by my tree." I didn't really want a buttercup chain but I was running out of ideas about what to do with my none-too-bright prisoner.

She did exactly as she was told and then went and sat back down in her former spot.

"What's your name?"

"Melissa, but everyone calls me Missy. I'm almost seven."

"*I'm almost seven,*" I mocked her in a baby lisp, even though I was starting to feel a little bad about how mean I was being. "What're you doing here, Missy?"

"Just visiting my granddaddy. Mama let us outside to play for a while."

As if summoned by Missy's words, her mama appeared at the screen door calling out, "Y'all come on in now and say goodbye to granddaddy." The two boys started turning somersaults and cartwheels in the direction of the house. "Missy! Come on in," the mother yelled louder.

Missy turned to look at me and I felt the power of the gun in my hand, "You're my prisoner. You don't go till I say you can go."

The panic in the girl's face both elated and shamed me.

"Missy Sinclair! You better get your scrawny hide over here right this minute." Her mother was coming down the steps in our direction.

"Not till I say so," I hissed again.

Missy plucked at the grass around her and seemed to tear up but stayed planted. When it was clear her mother was going to keep advancing on us, I said as calmly as I could, "OK. You can go. But walk, don't run. Remember, I got a gun on you."

Missy got up and walked stiffly towards her mother who was looking red in the face. When she got close enough her mother grabbed her by the shoulder and started shaking her hard.

"Girl, didn't you hear me calling you? You dragging your feet like dead lice 'bout to fall off you. What's got into you!"

"I couldn't move," Missy whimpered.

"What you mean you couldn't move?" her mother demanded.

"I was a prisoner. A mean girl back there was pointing a gun at me."

"What in Lord's name are you talking about?"

"That girl by the tree, she was pointing a gun at me and made me give her my buttercup necklace and said I was her prisoner and not to come when you called me," Missy hiccupped.

Her mother looked up and around. I held my breath and stayed behind the tree, gearing up in case I'd need to make a dash for it. Then the woman hauled off and slapped Missy full on the face, the sound so sharp it stung my ears.

"You better quit your foolishness, making up stories like that when you ain't minding. Lying tongues is straight from the Devil. You keep that up and I'll tan your hide good, just see if I don't."

Missy was crying and hiccupping as her mother jerked her along by the arm toward the house, but she didn't say anything else about being a prisoner.

When the screen door slammed shut, I stayed frozen behind the tree, looking down at the buttercup chain near my feet. I inched it closer to me with the gun barrel and squatted slowly to pick it up. *No evidence,* I thought. I backed up towards the woods behind me, careful to keep the tree trunk between myself and the house at all times. Back in the woods I walked softly, even after I was long out of earshot of the farmhouse. When I got near our backyard, I dug a hole in the soft dirt, tore the buttercup chain into tiny pieces, and dropped it in. I palmed the dirt over it, patted it down, and wiped my buttercup-yellowed fingers and dirty hands off on my shirt.

That Boy Rather Dance

When the Good Samaritan program started at Sunday School, I felt sick with dread. This was exactly the sort of thing I hated most, pretending to be good for long stretches, doing things you don't want to do in order to help thy neighbor. No way to get out of it without Mother and Daddy finding out either, since Miss Jean would be sure to tell. One of the first things Miss Jean mentioned was visiting the old folks' home to read or talk to the old people. Now, I've been to that place. My Aunt Gertie lives there and I can safely say it is the stinkiest place on earth. It smells like pee and Pine Sol, enough combined ammonia to leave you gagging and dizzy. If that's not bad enough, the old people wander around shaking and talking to themselves, that's the ones that ain't lying in bed moaning like they're dying—which they just might be. It's a creepy, awful place. Aunt Gertie, from Birdy's side of the family, had her own room there, but she wasn't too bad off. She was pretty normal really, and it had occurred to me to feel sorry for her, being stuck in there. Instead of smelling like most old people, she reeked of Eau de Toilette. Cracks me up. Eau de Toilette. She even called it toilet water. I could hardly keep from laughing out loud when she said it. Douses herself in it every day. She still talked sense, only in a froggy voice. She didn't wet her bed, thank the Lord, and she had her own bathroom. So, it wouldn't be horrible if I had to sit in her room to earn my gold star on the Good Samaritan board. I don't really remember when I first put two and two together, but it came to me at some point that Aunt Gertie would know about Billy. She would have been alive when he was killed. And without Birdy there to throw her off, she might be led to ramble on about the whole thing. It's like that old saying, *killing two birds with one stone:* I could get my gold star *and* maybe I could finally find out what really happened to Billy, the boy who'd rather dance than eat when he was hungry.

Walking down the hall toward her room, number 23, I peeked into the other rooms along the way. Aunt Gertie had a private room, but most of the rooms had two people in them, and some had three people crammed in together. They all seemed jam-packed with stuff—framed pictures, crosses, and whatnots. Curtains hung between the beds, looking more like faded sheets than real curtains. When I got to Aunt Gertie's door I knocked softly, waited, then knocked harder. Her voice was quavery but easy to hear, "Who is it?"

"It's Willie. Willie Miller, ma'am."

Long pause.

"Oh, Wilhelmina. Walter's girl. Come on in, dear."

A wave of Eau de Toilette hit me when I opened the door, but it was better than the hallway smell.

"Hi, Aunt Gertie. I came to talk to you."

"Did you now? Where are your folks?"

"They dropped me off for an hour so I could do my . . . so I could visit."

"So you could do some sort of penance? Am I your punishment?"

Her eyes were sharper than I remembered. She was sitting in a chair by the window, wearing a blue dress with a lighter blue sweater that had a crocheted collar. Her nylons were smooth, unwrinkled even at the ankles, and her shoes were low-heeled but dressy. She didn't look anything like the ladies shuffling around in robes and slippers in the day room.

On the tray in front of her, cards were lined up in columns, while she held about half the pack in her hand. We weren't allowed to play cards. It hit me again that Birdy's family was different than mine, even though we were the same family.

"No ma'am. It's just that at Sunday School we have to do our Good Samaritan deed. When we finish, Miss Jean puts a gold star by our name on the attendance board."

"Oh, yes," she put a card on a column. "Visit the elderly and infirm. Well, if you're going to read scripture to me, you may as well just turn right around and march yourself down to the day room to deliver the gospel to those good souls. I'm otherwise occupied."

I didn't remember her being so crotchety.

"No ma'am. I didn't bring my Bible."

"Well, praise Jesus!" She cackled. "So, what shall we discuss then, dear?"

A million scenarios flitted through my head, but before I could settle on a roundabout way, I blurted out, "Billy."

"Who?"

"Billy, my grand-uncle Billy."

"Girl," she put down the cards and looked squarely at me, "he died long before you were ever born. Why on God's green earth would you want to talk about him?"

"I don't know much about him."

"That boy'd rather dance than eat when he was hungry."

There it was again. The thing they always say about him, as if that were the most important feature of his story, not the fact that he died, maybe even got himself killed in a knife fight when he was a teenager.

"That's why he went to the juke joint that night, weren't it? He wanted to dance."

"*Wasn't* it."

"Huh? Oh, yes ma'am. Wasn't it." She was just like Birdy about talking. Birdy hated that me and Dare sounded country when we talked. She didn't come right out and say it, but I knew from the way she was constantly trying to fix our words. Seemed like Aunt Gertie felt the same way.

"He probably went there to dance."

She gave me an eagle eye stare until I had to look down at my Keds. Old people ought to be easier to talk to than this. I was used to the ones at church, patting my head, slipping me a nickel, saying *sweet girl.* They were easy to get a handle on. I didn't remember Aunt Gertie being so much not like an old lady. Then again, I never really talked directly to her. I came to visit sometimes with Birdy, or at Easter with Mother and Daddy, but the grown-ups did the talking.

"You want to know how he died."

I almost jumped out of my skin, but managed to nod.

"Well that is the million-dollar question. Join the club, little sister."

I returned her gaze.

"You don't know? But you're old enough . . . I mean, you were there, right?"

"Well, I wasn't at the juke joint, if that's your question, missy. But, yes, I was alive and well when Billy died."

She gave me another long stare, but I was ready this time and didn't look away.

"You apparently know enough to be curious, which leads me to believe you know he didn't die of natural causes, as they say. The unnatural causes were clear, but how they happened remains a mystery. Why do you wish to delve into this old business from before you were born?"

"He's still my family."

She sat back slightly, her lips closed but hinting at a smile.

"Yes. He's still your family, from a side you can be proud of."

She was doing that thing grown-ups do, where they say something that means more than it appears to mean. I wasn't about to be distracted, though. I could feel that the story was close, so I just waited.

"Billy was a free spirit before people used that term much, and before that sort of thing was much tolerated. Girls loved him. So did boys, for that matter. But that kind of charm can also get you in a lot of hot water. Billy lived a charmed life, too, getting out of everything scot-free, had his ma and poppa wrapped around his finger. Birdy adored him and trailed after him everywhere like he was her own personal Pied Piper. Poor girl."

She gathered up the cards, rapped the edges on the tray table until they were even, then placed them in the corner.

"Billy got into some sort of trouble, that much is certain." She said looking me in the eye. I looked right back.

She continued, "Birdy wouldn't talk about it and that's why you're asking me, isn't it? That and your little Good Samaritan badge."

"We don't get a badge, just a gold star on the attendance board."

"Christians distributing gold stars. Oh, that's rich!"

I had no idea what she meant, but I wasn't going to let her change the subject.

"Birdy said everyone loved Billy. But it seems like somebody didn't. I mean, everyone keeps hinting how he was beat up or something, maybe worse, maybe a knife fight."

She stiffened. "Who said that?"

"No one. Just seems like, that's all."

"Wilhelmina, no one is trying to hide the truth from you. The truth is, no one knows for sure. Believe me, Sheriff Dixon questioned everyone multiple times, even folks who weren't there that night. The boys he went out there with had been drinking and none of their stories matched up. Whether they were covering for him or themselves or both, only God knows. The facts won't help you, honey, but if you want them, I'll tell you."

"Yes," was all I could squeak out.

She sat back a little again, getting comfortable, I suppose. "Billy was found in a car that had rolled and landed in a ditch on Old County Road. No one was with him. It was a friend's car, one of the boys he'd gone out there with. They were all buddies from Roosevelt High School. When the sheriff found him, he was slung over the front seat, like he'd been trying to crawl into the back seat, but hadn't made it. His face was bruised, he had broken ribs, and he was bloody from puncture wounds. I didn't see his body, but I heard all about it at the kitchen table before everybody stopped speaking of it. Billy had gone out there with three friends, but was all alone when the sheriff found him. He was already dead. My big brother Ash, Billy's daddy, your great-grandfather, knew Sheriff Dixon well. They took hunting trips together. The sheriff brought Billy back to their house, not to a morgue or hospital or any place where strangers might touch him. He could have lost his job for that, but back then folks understood that sometimes you have to bend the rules to do what's right. Mama was one of the women that helped lay him out the next day, and maybe where the talk of knives came from. She said his cuts looked like ice pick wounds, not anything that might happen in a rolled car. The sheriff questioned all those boys early that morning. Two of them were at their homes. All these boys still lived with their folks, you see, so you can imagine the ruckus. And the third one, piece of filth that he was, Sheriff Dixon found sleeping it off down at the migrant workers' camp—not alone either."

She shot me a sharp look.

"Why did the boys leave him? If he was in one of their cars then how did they get home?"

"Wilhelmina, the pint-sized girl detective," she smiled. "That's just one of many questions the sheriff asked over and over for months until finally, Ash, himself, convinced Dixon to drop it and close the case, ruling it an accidental death."

Aunt Gertie looked out the window for a few minutes before she continued.

"The sheriff talked to Billy's friends before those boys had a chance to get their stories straight. The first one claimed that Billy borrowed the car in order to give a girl a ride back to Feral, but he was gone so long the other three started walking back toward town and ended up walking all the way home without seeing him. The car was rolled in the other direction, not toward town, so they wouldn't have seen him. But that story clearly wasn't entirely true since only two of them made it back to their own beds that night; that other one was rolling around like a dog in the dirt at the migrant camp. The second boy the sheriff talked to said the three of them hitched a ride with a stranger that was passing by and, no, they didn't get his name or a good look at the car. And if that wasn't fishy enough, he didn't seem to know that only two of them had made it back to town either. That no account boy, Wesley, claimed to have blacked out, only recollecting being at the juke joint. The trollop at the camp where the sheriff found him apparently had no clearer memory of the night either. Worthless trash."

She paused again, looking out the window. Her face had a soft sort of hanging look that it hadn't had earlier.

"Thing is, there were rumors about Billy even before that night. Maybe it was just jealousy like Birdy says, but maybe there was some truth in them, too. Some folks said it was more than dancing that he liked, more intimate pursuits. Who knows? He was a good-looking boy. People love to gossip, though, and a rumor started that he'd gotten some country girl in trouble. That was just one of the rumors. Everybody in town was talking about poor Billy, speculating on what happened out there on Old County Road, how maybe he'd been killed, and it was made to look like a car accident on account of him getting a girl in trouble. That's when that piece of filth Wesley said what he did, said Billy would have been better off if he had stuck to girls instead of going off with a boy. Who'd listen to a scoundrel who admits to being a blackout drunk, who rolls around with trash in a migrant worker shack? But it was like he struck a match to dry kindling. It was like wildfire that sordid lie, whispered around from high to low."

She was frowning and shaking her head. She looked smaller in her careful blue dress, frail.

"Blackout, my foot. He probably got into the mischief he was speaking of and needed to drag Billy down to his level somehow. May he rot in hell."

She jerked her head toward me then, suddenly quiet.

I smiled to let her know I didn't mind about the cussing. But the story didn't make sense. I knew what happened when girls got in trouble. It meant they were going to have a baby when they weren't married yet, like that Tidewater girl that Ricky had to marry. But what had made Aunt Gertie so mad was what the boy said about Billy going off with another boy, which should have cleared him. That meant he wasn't getting a girl in trouble like they said. Maybe the boy was lying, trying to cover for Billy, but that didn't explain why Aunt Gertie would get cussing mad.

"If he went off with a boy, then he wasn't getting a girl in trouble. . . ." I trailed off, hoping she would see the sense in this.

She looked at me for a long time. I was starting to think that maybe she was asleep with her eyes open, because she got this unfocused sort of stare like she was looking right through me, like she was seeing something else, not me.

"No. If he had been with a boy, he wouldn't have been getting a girl in trouble. You're right about that, Wilhelmina." She said it in a low, tired voice. She sounded so sad it was like she had just heard he was dead.

I moved my chair around the tray table to sit next to her, feeling somehow protective.

"That's good, right? I'm sorry it happened." I didn't really know what to say, or why I felt like I needed to comfort her.

She pulled her sweater more tightly around herself, even though the room had grown warmer, not cooler.

"It was a long time ago, honey. Whatever Billy was, he was loved. And he was a good boy, a sweet boy, kind-hearted as could be. He didn't deserve it. He didn't deserve to go like that. He was smart enough to go to any good college. He had a future. Then he didn't . . . then he didn't."

She shook her head and turned back to the window.

The sadness in the room wrapped around everything. I felt like I couldn't move because the air had gotten too heavy. Aunt Gertie's jaw was quivering. With an effort, I got up and stood by her. She wasn't like the church ladies who hugged all the time, and somehow I knew she was off in her own place somewhere, and it didn't matter that I was there. So, I waited. After a while, she turned back towards where I stood, but looked past me.

"It's all ancient history now, Wilhelmina. What good is it to bring up again?" Her voice cracked a little.

The heavy weight in my chest dropped to my stomach. I was supposed to be doing a good deed. I was going to get a gold star for it. And here I was bringing misery to my old Aunt Gertie, bringing up things I'd been told over and over not to talk about. Billy was dead. It hit me now that he was real to Birdy and to Aunt Gertie, the way Dare was real to me; not a story, but a person, a real person. A brother. A nephew. My throat tightened and I hated myself for being so selfish. I leaned over awkwardly and kissed Aunt Gertie's dry, powdery cheek. She looked up at me steadily, not frowning or smiling, not patting my hand or saying *sweet girl*, just a long, thoughtful stare. Then she said, "Willie, you don't need anyone to give you a gold star. Hear me, girl? You go on being just who you are, and as long as you don't hurt anyone, who you are is just fine."

Tears burned at my eyes and I couldn't swallow. It's awful when you've been mean or selfish and then that person turns around and is soft to you.

"You go ahead and let them put that gold star on the wall, but just keep this thought in your heart, Willie, that star isn't what's important. Only your own stars, Willie. Don't you forget that."

Dog Days

After one of my sleepovers at Birdy's, she took me to the city park to spend the day before driving me back home to the country. I loved the park, especially the concession stand where they sold snow cones. Birdy was talking to some town ladies on a shady bench at the far end of the park. I made my way towards her, sucking the cherry syrup from the rounded top of my snow cone. In the parking lot, just inside the gate, I saw a clump of boys on bikes. Almost instantly, I recognized Dare. I heard one of the boys say, "That your sister or your brother?" as I came near. The sneer in his voice was unmistakable.

"Screw you, Murphy," Dare said.

At least I could still count on him to be on my side.

I got close enough that I could smell their boy smell, a coppery sweat musk with a whiff of tobacco. I wished they would all fall into a crater and die and leave Dare there with me, so we could go down to the river again where the little kids fed ducks stale Wonder Bread. But he was with them now, not even looking at me.

"Hey Dare."

He didn't even say hey back.

The boys just looked around like I wasn't there. The tall one, Murphy, spat on the pavement.

"Dad says this park is closing before the integration." Murphy didn't seem to say this to anyone in particular. No one answered and we all just sort of stood there, looking off in no fixed direction.

"Goddamn niggers going to spoil everything." Murphy spat again.

I felt my face flush and my heart began to pound in my ears. I turned my head to Dare to see how he was going to fix it. It wasn't just the bad words, it was all of it. But Dare was looking off into the distance like he hadn't seen or heard.

I looked back at Murphy. Like all the boys, he was resting on his bike seat with one foot on the ground, the other on his pedal. His sneer made me want to kick him hard.

"Goddamn niggers," he repeated.

"Jerk." My throat was so dry that when the sound creaked out, it was a squeak. At first, it seemed like no one heard. Then Murphy aimed his eyes my way.

"What'd you say?"

I dropped my eyes. But then it came up even stronger, like when you try not to vomit but it busts out anyway. "You're a big, fat jerk." This time loud.

"Look guys, it can talk. Hey, you a boy or a girl? Or maybe a hermaphrodite, huh?"

I glanced back to see where Birdy was. She was still sitting with the town ladies across the park. I didn't look at Dare.

"That it? You a hermaphrodite?"

"Lay off," Dare said.

"What's it to you?" Murphy turned toward Dare.

"Nothing. She's a kid is all."

"Hey, kid. What's your problem anyway?" He turned back to me.

I glared at him. His ugly pink face, and fingers with dirt under the nails wrapped around his handlebars, made my stomach churn. I wanted to knock him off his bike and kick his face bloody.

"Good riddance to hermaphrodites and niggers, I say. This park is for shit-eaters." He started to turn his bike around back towards the street and something inside me broke.

I don't know what I was going to do, but I lunged towards him, dropping my snow cone. Dare pedaled between us, looking hard at me. I stopped. Murphy turned around.

"What? Your little bitch sister going to attack me, Country? She some sort of nigger-loving hermaphrodite?"

"Stop saying that." Dare's teeth were clenched.

"Stop saying what? She's a hermaphrodite or a nigger-lover? Huh, Country?" Murphy spat.

In a movement so fast it didn't seem real, Dare's bike was down and he had Murphy on the ground. Dare was heavier, but Murphy was tall, all arms and legs. I'd never seen Dare punch anyone, but he was punching Murphy in the stomach, face, anywhere he could land a blow. The other boys circled their bikes around them. Still, a man across the parking lot started over our way yelling, "Break it up, boys." I craned around trying to spot Birdy, to see whether she had noticed the ruckus, but she was still on the park bench, facing safely away from us. If she saw Dare fighting in a parking lot, he'd be in a world of trouble. When I turned back, Dare and Murphy were clambering back on their bikes. The rest of the gang was already peeling out of the parking lot. The man, red-faced and huffing, slowed, then just stood there, staring at their retreating bodies. It all seemed to happen in fast motion. They were gone in a blink. My snow cone was melting into a small red puddle on the pavement. I slunk back to the park grounds, and when I was almost in her blind spot, I ran toward Birdy.

"Birdy! Did you see that? There were some Feral boys fighting in the parking lot!" I had her looking at me. In fact, she was looking at me a little too closely.

"Where have you been, Willie?"

I pointed toward the river. "Looking at the ducks. We forgot to bring bread."

She didn't answer. Her friends were drifting off. She looked around and so did I. The boys in the parking lot were long gone.

Birdy stood up, glancing down at me. "Are you ready to go?"

"Yes ma'am."

At home that night, when we sat down to supper, Dare avoided looking at me. He didn't look bruised up or anything, and it didn't seem like he was in any trouble. Mother asked me if I had a good time at Birdy's, and I said I did without mentioning we went to the city park. Dare didn't say anything.

Later, before we went to bed, I knocked on Dare's bedroom door.

"What?"

"Can I come in?"

"What for?"

I came in and sat on the spare bed that used to be Granddaddy's. I didn't really know what I'd come in to say. I had a knot in the pit of my stomach.

"That guy Murphy is a jerk. Why do you hang out with him?"

"You're a jerk. Go to bed."

"What was that name he called me? Hermfrodite? And how come you didn't say nothing when he said 'nigger,' you just acted like you didn't hear?"

"Get out of here. I don't have to explain nothing to you."

I felt that sharp flare of anger, but then it sort of fizzled. If I didn't have Dare, what did I even have? I was fighting back tears and they sounded in my voice.

"How come? How come you let him talk like that to me, Dare?"

He flew off the bed, grabbed me by the shoulder and pushed me toward the door.

"Go on. Get."

I was standing in his doorway, like so many times before. His face was close to mine and he was frowning, but he looked shaky.

"Why did you even have to be there today? You ruined everything. Go on. Go to bed and leave me alone." He slammed the door.

I didn't even turn the light on in my room. I hadn't ruined everything. Murphy had. Then I knew that Dare was going to stick with him, even though he had knocked him off his bike and punched him. He was going to choose Murphy, the jerk. Not me.

The Boy

Miss Alma was the first to come over, the first voice I heard to begin the story. I knew something big was up because when we heard her car in the driveway, Mother started wiping her hands with a dish towel and said, "Reckon I better make a *big* pot of coffee," with such a deep sigh that I already had a hunch somebody died or something just as bad had happened. She did that thing where she straightened up like she was getting ready for something that she needed to fix her mind on, like when she killed snakes in the garden with a hoe.

Miss Alma barely had the bag full of apples on the counter before she started talking. Before Mother even had a chance to tell me to get outside and play, I was out the door. The dirt was cool and the Nandina bush gave me some shade, the dappled light shifting as I sat down, leaning my back against the house, drawing my knees up.

Miss Alma had been talking for several minutes already about the boy, but when I settled in I heard her say "Hung him from a tree out there and whether it was birds or what they done, his eyes were out. . . ." my stomach turned over. Maybe I hadn't heard her right. But she kept on. "Now, I can't tell you whether it's true about being drug behind a pickup, but I know for a fact that his people were the ones that came and cut him down and carried him off. He's in that colored funeral home just over in Chesapeake. I heard they're keeping the coffin open for the viewing, which if you ask me is just going to rile them up."

"Alma," Mother's voice was flinty, a tone she never took with the church ladies, "I'm sure everyone is already riled up, like they ought to be. Grown men killed a boy."

"Well," Miss Alma huffed. "I'm certainly not making excuses for anyone, but no smoke without fire, as they say."

"A boy, Alma. A fifteen-year-old boy. Same age as one of your own. No one even seems to know what really happened aside from some drunken fools waylaid the boy and ended up killing him on account of some hearsay."

"Maybe hearsay and maybe not. I'm sure someone knows what happened and I trust our own kind to do what needs to be done."

I could hear a chair scrape the floor. Mother's voice was further away when I heard her say, "Well, I don't think of drunken killers as my people. Do you want some more coffee?" Her voice was cold and flat, the offer clearly not genuine.

Then I heard Miss Alma's chair scrape.

"No thank you, Mary. My nerves are jangled. I should probably just go into town and get my groceries."

I didn't know Miss Alma well enough to figure out what the high pitch in her words meant, whether she was insulted or apologetic. I'd never heard Mother be rude to any of the church ladies before, and it added to the queasy feeling in my stomach. I put my chin on my knees and shut my eyes. They had moved to the front of the house and before long I heard the gravel under Miss Alma's tires and knew she was gone. I could hear my mother back in the kitchen, moving around, putting things away. This was what I always wanted, to find out those things the grown-ups kept from us, their secret stories. But I wished I hadn't heard this. The sick feeling got worse as I pictured a boy hanging from a tree, where grown men had hung him, maybe men I had seen somewhere in town, maybe even men I knew. I thought about Mr. Armstrong, about all the men who had come to help put out the fire I'd started in the woods. Unimaginable. What about Miss Alma's husband? He hardly ever came to church. He had a pickup. The baggy man at Culpepper's flashed across my mind. I couldn't stop the thoughts, but I couldn't let them keep going either. There were other parts, too, that I couldn't let in yet—his eyes, the before time, before he was dead. It was too much to hold in. I made my way quietly out from under the bush so Mother wouldn't hear, but when I got to the side yard I started to run. I circled the house until I was heading back towards the woods, running as fast as I could, but the thoughts and images kept flashing up: the boy in the tree, Miss Alma's soft voice, drunk white men, my mother squaring her shoulders, a pickup truck, the boy in the tree, the boy in the tree. As I crashed through the woods, branches whipped my arms and legs. I ducked under low limbs, but I wouldn't slow down. Finally, when I got near the Sample farmland, I threw myself under a huge oak, panting. The sick feeling stayed in my gut, but I didn't throw up. Miss Alma had said *our own kind* like we should stick up for the killers. I knew it was because they were white and the boy was colored. I lay back looking at the play of light and shadow through the interlaced branches above me and there he was. I closed my eyes and there he was. He would never be gone, that boy hung from a tree. *Not my kind,* I thought, *they will never be my kind.*

Suffer the Little Children

The first sound I heard was the chainsaw from the back woods, then birds loud in the trees. The morning breeze felt good coming through the screen, faintly scented with gardenia. I usually liked lying in bed daydreaming before getting up, but today the image of the killed boy came back almost immediately, and with it the sick feeling that wouldn't go away. For the past few days Mother seemed to know something was wrong, every now and then putting her hand on my forehead, or asking me if I had a stomach ache.

The church ladies had swarmed the house, buzzing endlessly as cicadas. I had quit eavesdropping, even though they sometimes embroidered the story with new details.

I couldn't listen anymore. Before I fell asleep at night, the caves where his eyes should have been stared at me. He wasn't from here, and I really hoped, I hoped with all my heart that neither were the men. But they were from somewhere close. And they had killed him. They had tortured and killed him. It made the whole world a different place. Even after days of riding my bike pondering, I couldn't make any sense of it. I avoided riding by Shillin Town as much as possible, knowing I'd look like someone from an enemy camp to anyone coming or going from there. I couldn't face Miss Alma in church because as nice as she was, she said those things about the integration, and then she stood up for the boy's killers. No one said his name and I wondered if they knew it or if that, too, had been killed with him. Days felt heavy and all I wanted was for it to go back to the before time, when even the idea of a boy being killed by grown-ups would be ridiculous, impossible even. But I knew it wouldn't go back.

When I had tried to solve the mystery of Billy's death, it

was like a game or a book, where I was the center, figuring things out, putting the story together. I was a long way from the center, now. I knew that. The boy who got killed, where was his family? Did he have a sister who loved him the way Birdy still loved Billy? If it were Dare who had been killed, I would spend my life hunting those men down and I would kill them. I would. Every single one. I couldn't stop thinking of it and, as I often had, I wished I didn't know. I wished the grown-ups had kept their secret so that I would never see that hanging boy with eye caves again, whether in my sleep or when I was awake.

Later in the morning I rode towards Feral, but turned off before town at Lake Gardens Cemetery. Willows swept gracefully beside a small man-made lake. Gravel lanes made a web of connection around the gravesites and stone houses, through the perfectly manicured lawn. I had never thought of cemeteries as being white or black, but I now realized only white people came to this one, kneeling with flowers, or trimming grass back from headstones. Where had they taken him? The ladies said that his family came to "cut him down" and take him away. Did his dad climb a ladder up the tree and saw through the rope? Did they let him drop on the ground, or was there someone there to catch him? And how was any of it even possible? I tried to imagine my father cutting me or Dare down from a tree and I just couldn't.

Lying my bike on the ground, I settled under one of the willows and ran my fingers through the dirt and grass to find pebbles to throw in the lake. I tossed them one at a time, a sad plop followed by widening ripples. The cemetery was quiet. Except for birds, I seemed to be the only living thing here. Finally, I could cry.

I let tears pour down my face, not even caring. They were for Birdy when Billy got killed, they were for Granddaddy because I'd simply forgotten him as if he had never lived with us, they were for me because Dare had left me and I was lost without him. But mostly they were for him, a boy I would never know, who was killed by grown-ups, the people kids rely on to help and protect us. I knew he was killed for being colored, and that he could have never been anything else, no matter how hard he tried.

I cried until I gasped for air and had to blow snot into my shirt. Finally exhausted, I put my head on my knees. *Everything has changed,* I thought. Then, as a mourning dove took back up its low refrain, I thought *maybe it was always this way.* But I wasn't even sure what that meant. I knew there was no going back. I couldn't unknow this. And I couldn't separate the killed boy from Miss Alma and from church and from Jesus who said *suffer the little children unto me,* something I'd always thought of as *let the kids come sit in my lap* because of the picture in Sunday School that had that scripture as caption. Why didn't God stop those killers?

The crying had been like a storm and I felt tired and empty. As the snot started to dry and crust in my shirt, I thought *I'm never moving from this spot. I'm just going to sit here forever.* When my butt started to ache, I realized it was a stupid thought, as if I were two years old instead of ten. My stomach growled.

I lifted my bike from the grass, surveying the rows of white tombstones like a frozen flock of granite birds. Acres of the dead fanned out in perfect conformity on carefully planned plots. I liked the tiny Sample graveyard better, with its rusted wrought iron fencing and decrepit graves, where everyone was related and haphazardly squeezed in. It was peaceful here, though. The sky was so blue and the clouds pillowy, the kind of sky that makes you think of heaven. I felt like there was a crack growing in my picture of God and heaven, though. Still, I hoped, hoped hard, that heaven was like they'd said, a place of peace that surpasses understanding, where God's eternal love lifts us from all misery and the endless day is full of joy. I hoped the boy was there and that with his own eyes, he saw God.

Pedal

Of the two deaths that summer, one buried deep in the past, the other brutally present, it was the latter that would haunt me, even though I never knew him, not even his name. I heard the boy and his family lived in Mill Creek, just over the state line, where he'd been killed. I sometimes thought of him as *the other Billy* even though I knew that wasn't right.

Most mornings I still lit out on my bike right after breakfast. I hit the blacktop toward the Dismal Swamp, fields and farmland on either side of the road. I dropped my arms to my sides. Was it only last summer I had learned to ride hands free? I could do it for long stretches now, not just uncertain seconds with my hands carefully hovering above the handlebars, ready to grab ahold at any shaky moment.

I pedaled on with my arms by my sides, as if no holding on would ever again be necessary, legs in a fast-paced pump. The smell of pine needles baking in the sun, cool green moments of shade, the oil slick rainbow some grease spot made on the pavement, crickets clicking—everything moved past and through me. I felt like I would always be riding down this road, with a long summer stretching out, pointing toward an inevitable fall, bobwhites repeating overhead. I pedaled faster, as if to escape, or as if a prize lay ahead. I lifted my scrawny arms out like wings. The sun at my back cast a long shadow ahead that looked for all the world like a girl in flight.

Acknowledgements

Thank you to the editors and journals that published individual stories from *Feral, North Carolina, 1965*:

Bartleby Snopes: "Nighttime Stories"; *Belle Rêve*: "Beloved Angel" & "Church Ladies" (nominated for a Pushcart); *Big Muddy*: "Firebug"; *Deep South Magazine*: "Dare" (originally titled "In Fairfield, On Earth"); P*er Contra*: "Winning Prisoner"; *Santa Fe Writers Project*: "Buttercup Chain" (reprint, included in an inaugural anthology); *Steel Toe Review*: "Shooting for the Lead" (originally titled "Taking the Lead"); *The Village Rambler*: "Rapture" (originally titled "Left Behind"); *Third Wednesday*: "Buttercup Chain."

Heartfelt thanks to Pinckney Benedict, Steve McCondichie, April Ford, and the entire crew at Southern Fried Karma for believing in this book and guiding it into print. Endless gratitude to my lifelong mentor, Peter Makuck. Sincere thanks to many reader-friends who supported this work along the way: Robin Griffin, Gayle Brandeis, David Weaver, Nicole Victor, Mitch Boxberger, Marisella Veiga, Patricia Smith, Kim Wyatt, Brian Turner, Aydelette Isgar, Allison Hilborn, Suzanne Roberts, Krista Lukas, Michelle Palacio, Shannon Beets, Dan O'Bryan, Kim Bateman, Lori Longo, Leslie Oldershaw, Brian Hobbs (rest in peace, old friend), and others.

About the Author

June Sylvester Saraceno comes from a family of storytellers—sea-faring folk, preachers, coffee-fueled aunties, and good-time gabbers. Her stories harken back to her days growing up in the South, and she hopes to make her readers laugh, feel nostalgic, and recognize some of themselves. *Feral, North Carolina, 1965* is her first novel.

Photo by Carolina Cruz Guimarey

Share Your Thoughts

Want to help make *Feral, North Carolina, 1965* a bestselling novel? Consider leaving an honest review on Goodreads, your personal author website or blog, and anywhere else readers go for recommendations. It's our priority at SFK Press to publish books for readers to enjoy, and our authors appreciate and value your feedback.

Our Southern Fried Guarantee

If you wouldn't enthusiastically recommend one of our books with a 4- or 5-star rating to a friend, then the next story is on us. We believe that much in the stories we're telling. Simply email us at pr@sfkmultimedia.com.

Also by SFK Press

A Body's Just as Dead, Cathy Adams (2018)
Not All Migrate, Krystyna Byers (2019)
The Banshee of Machrae, Sonja Condit (2018)
Amidst This Fading Light, Rebecca Davis (2018)
American Judas, Mickey Dubrow (2018)
Swapping Purples for Yellows, Matthew Duffus (2019)
A Curious Matter of Men with Wings, F. Rutledge Hammes (2018)
The Skin Artist, George Hovis (2019)
Lying for a Living, Steve McCondichie (2017)
The Parlor Girl's Guide, Steve McCondichie (2019)
Appalachian Book of the Dead, Dale Neal (2019)
Hardscrabble Road, George Weinstein (2018)
Aftermath, George Weinstein (2018)
The Five Destinies of Carlos Moreno, George Weinstein (2018)
The Caretaker, George Weinstein (2019)
RIPPLES, Evan Williams (2019)

Made in the USA
San Bernardino,
CA

58819608R00090